First and Only

Destiny

GLORIA SILK

Cover Designed by Linda le Breten of LLB Studio
Interior Design by Woven Red Formatting Services, www.wovenred.ca

First and Only Destiny/Gloria Silk—1st edition
ISBN: 978-0-9936952-3-0

*To Austin and Natalia, my two constant loves.
Thank you for your support in so many ways.*

Acknowledgments

This story is the culmination of my long awaited dream of seeing my fiction come to life, and hopefully, to be shared with readers all over the world.

Huge thanks to *all* the effervescent members of the Quince Apple Group, and especially to Storm Grant, Joan Leacott, and Bonnie Staring, and with heart-felt gratitude to my long-time mentor and friend, Kate Freiman. Thanks for all your graceful patience, your sense of fun, and insightful critiques and discussions.

Also thanks to my reading and writing team of friends: Yvonne Finn, Bethea Reznik, Anya Richards, Mike Spiers, Alan Stuart, Stella Yosefi. Warm thanks go to my two smart and amazing new adult editors, Natalia Freedman and Anna Hardcastle. All your advice and encouragement has been invaluable, as always.

Of course, thank you to others who also helped make my work so much better over the years.

Finally, my love and appreciation to my own personal hero, Austin—without whose unfailing support my dreams would not come true—and other loved ones, who have been so encouraging and helpful along my journey to being published.

Author's Note

This is an extensive, stand-alone prequel to SECOND DESTINY, telling the story of how Lia and Devraj first meet at a London university. It explains how love changes their young lives forever and how and why their combined and separate decisions mold their futures and completely alter their destiny.

Glossary

Chuppa (hu-pa)	Wedding Canopy (Hebrew)
Maharajah	A ruling prince (Hindi)
Rabbi	Preacher/Reverend (Hebrew)
Rajah	A king or prince in India (Hindi)
Rani	Queen (Hindi)

Prologue

North London, June 1995

LEAVING THE TOMB-LIKE silence of the Rolls Royce, Lia gripped the heavy skirt of her imprisoning wedding dress, while accepting the stooping, old man's help to brave the summer downpour.

The big, bat-like umbrella over them absorbed the mini bullets of the rain, turning the pure white of her gown to gunmetal gray.

Was it sunrise or sunset? She couldn't remember. The universe had lost all color and warmth.

Her feet and heart refused to cooperate as the old man tightened his embrace around her and urged her toward the arched doors of the imposing granite-grey building ahead of them.

A familiar magnetic pull made her turn her head to look over her shoulder, across the road. Lips trembling under the stifling veil, she saw the soaking, unshaven, Devraj standing by his car.

She felt his agony, heard his thoughts, *How can you throw away your life, our destiny? Please come back to me!*

But the sleek, dark river of the London street may as well have been oceans separating them, like a chasm of culture neither could overcome.

Even if she was making the mistake of a lifetime, she needed him to see her enter the house of her God. Her first love was an illusion and a part of her past, now. He had to be.

Suddenly, thunder reverberated above them. She turned away from the love of her life. *Look forward, not back.*

"Love will come, you'll see. Howard will make you happy." Her grandmother's mantra over the past endless weeks had almost made Lia want to scream that it would only make her grandparents happy. But... here she was, still walking in the opposite direction from Devraj. For his own sake.

Whether or not he ever forgave her, one day she'd be proud of her strength and sacrifice.

Tears streaming down her face, she forced her legs up the stairs into the dimness. The cool, musty scent of the traditions ingrained into the spirit of the synagogue made her shiver.

Faces of curious strangers watched her advance towards the waiting bridegroom. The high jewel-tone stained-glass windows, to which generations of proud families had contributed, seemed about to shatter in on her. And, as every hesitant step led her closer to the man at the end of the aisle, his patent happiness made her steps falter, and she wanted to shout, *it's a lie; you know nothing about me!*

She almost stumbled, but Dedda supported her. The

nightmare continued.

But *this* was her destiny, not the heart-broken, young man out in the rain.

Statue-still, she lowered her burning eyes behind the veil. If Devraj ran up that aisle, demanding he was her rightful soul mate, would she flee with him? No!

Sucking in a shaky breath, she prayed for strength from the same God who'd gifted—and then snatched away—an alternate, impossible future.

Anchoring her limbs, she swore to be the perfect wife to the smiling man beside her. She wasn't marrying him for her grandparents, but for a much bigger reason.

Or—she raised her head, heart pounding—she could grab the long train of her white dress as restrictive as armor, and escape into the arms of her one and only true love.

She took another fortifying breath. Her fingers unfurled from their fists like opening petals.

Chapter One

University of Central London, eight months earlier

Lia stole another glance at the beautiful, exotic young man whose image she was trying to capture in her sketchpad. Trying to ignore the bustling atmosphere of the campus cafeteria, she focused on the sensuous feel of the charcoal stick within her shaking fingers, as it stroked the paper. Surreptitiously, she studied her subject's confident body language and his slightly amused, slightly superior expression, which acted on all her senses.

Once again, everything around her had faded to background noise as soon as she'd seen the tall, young man several yards away, standing with his friends, yet seeming to be apart from them.

What a perfect Rajah he would be, dignified and confident, waiting for his beautiful Hindi bride to appear. Lia imagined the delicate fragrance of a jasmine-and-rose wedding garland around his neck. She resisted the temptation to draw him in a traditional white-and-gold bridegroom's suit.

Why had she never met a "suitable" Jewish man who captured her imagination like this?

Suddenly, her subject turned away from the girl smiling up at him and looked straight at Lia. Immediately she glanced away from those bright hazel eyes. Heat flushed her cheeks and her shaking hand stilled above her sketch. Why had she chosen to draw him again? Was she watching too many Bollywood movies with her aunt and grandmother?

Compelled by fascination with the forbidden, Lia hesitantly lifted her head. She watched the young man stride towards her across the short span between them, his gaze never releasing hers.

She gulped, forgetting how to breathe.

Hunching over her sketchpad, she wished she could disappear. He wouldn't understand her interest in him was purely artistic.

Or was it?

Her world slowed as his bold steps covered the distance between them, like a conquering Maharaja with golden-dark skin claiming his bride. The charcoal stick snapped in half in her hand. A sense of inevitability rippled through her as he reached her table and she raised her head to look fully into his face.

Her many sketches hadn't done him justice.

Drawing in a revitalizing breath, she stared into those amber eyes that seemed to shine from within.

Lia absorbed his relaxed aura and easy-going smile, the tones of his skin, and the shiny black hair stroking his denim shirt collar. Even the slight bump on his regal nose added to his attraction.

His eyes lowered to her sketch.

With clammy, shaky hands, she snapped the pad shut but couldn't look away from him.

He rested one large, golden, beautifully shaped hand on the edge of the table and leaned toward her. "Like what you see?" in a rich baritone that caressed even as it teased.

"I don't know what you mean." Her face prickled, leaving her as hot as if sunburned. She probably looked as red as a cooked lobster.

Smile widening, he sat opposite her. "Let me see?" his tone a mix of request and demand she found arrogant ... and maybe a little attractive.

She clutched her sketchbook. "Absolutely not."

Her refusal didn't dim his smile. "Did you give me horns and crossed-eyes?"

Lia shook her head. "No, of course not! I mean it's... it's private."

He shrugged, studying her, "Well, it's my image you're using. I should be allowed to see what you've done."

She took a slow, steadying breath. "I ... I'm sorry. I won't sketch you anymore."

"I don't mind. In fact, I'm flattered. I just want to see—"

"Please leave me alone."

His dark brows rose. "Hey, now. That's not very friendly.

You seemed to be interested—"

"Please?" she interrupted softly, but clearly he heard her, because he stopped in mid-sentence and watched her reproachfully.

This was her own fault. She'd been staring at him, *drawing* him, for several days. Treating him as if he were a still life. But he was a live, healthy, attractive man, not a bowl of fruit, so of course he'd misunderstood.

She glanced at the group he'd left minutes earlier, several young men, as dazzlingly handsome as the hunks in Gillette adverts, and sophisticated girls draped next to them, all students, all strangers to her.

They'd gone silent, their eyes fixed on her with patent curiosity. Also obvious was the hostility in the narrowed eyes and flattened lips of one young blonde woman, fashionably dressed, boldly made up. Her confident and assertive body language proclaimed her a woman who belonged here, not intimidated and out of her depths, like Lia herself.

Heat penetrated from her neck up to her face as Lia shifted her gaze from the scrutiny of this man's friends and looked up only far enough to focus on his chin. "Please go away." In the silence that met her words, she suddenly heard how rude, how unfriendly she sounded.

Maybe if she explained. "I'm sorry, I-I'm here ... just to study. I'm not supposed to ... mingle."

She watched as he weighed her words, holding her breath, willing him to accept her explanation and simply retreat to his own world.

Instead, he grinned and shook his head. "I'm Devraj, but people call me Dev, or Dave." He reached out his hand. His long fingers drew her attention but she wasn't supposed to touch a man who wasn't family.

Devraj. Even his name was striking, regal. Feeling panicky because she *wanted* to touch his hand, wanted to feel his fingers on her own, Lia stood so quickly that her chair made a harsh noise against the floor.

Devraj stood up, too. Staring at him, Lia felt herself sway forward slightly and suddenly understood how magnetism worked. Grabbing her large cumbersome bag and draping it over her left shoulder she said, "I told you, I'm here, at this school, to study, not t-to ... meet strangers. I ... I have to go. Excuse me."

Her pulse galloping, Lia clutched her sketchbook to her chest and spun round to flee.

But he blocked her way.

Was he really being rejected? By this pretty little mouse of an artist? Dev laughed at his own astonishment and conceit.

Without thinking, he closed his fingers around one slender wrist. She gasped as if his touch had burned her, frightened her. Her eyes widened and she pulled back.

Feeling like a heel, he let go and replayed what she'd said to him. *She wasn't supposed to mingle? She was only here to study?*

Stepping back, he studied the trembling beauty in front of him. Dark hair, braided tightly down her back. White, long sleeved blouse buttoned up to her neck, the loosely wrapped skirt almost down to her flats. No liner or mascara on those dark, long lashed almond-shaped eyes, which were even more stunning at close range, and no lipstick on her soft, full lips.

His earlier boredom and restlessness disappeared. Adventure beckoned.

He'd felt her eying him before, admiring her sense of purpose and dogmatic passion. Now, her air of fragile self-preservation fascinated him. Her pale porcelain-fine skin had a rosy glow on her cheeks again, holding her sketchbook like a shield. He didn't want her to be afraid of him.

Dev didn't want her to feel she had to protect herself from him. No, he wanted to protect her. Not from himself—he'd never done, never would do, anything to hurt or endanger a woman—but from all the negative forces the world could throw at a sensitive, obviously sheltered artist. She was like an exquisite, wary hummingbird perched before him, poised to fly away.

He wanted to make her smile and relax her guard and stay.

"Don't run away. I'd like to get to know you. We have something in common. I'm an artist of sorts, too. Architecture. We could just sit and talk." He smiled carefully, not wanting to appear like the big bad wolf sizing up Little Red Riding Hood. "I'm really a nice guy, you know."

Bemused and unable to resist the sensation of falling under the spell of his velvety, seductive voice, Lia stared up at him and thought, *he's so tall.*

Clutching the pad tighter, she re-anchored the strap of her heavy bag on her shoulder. "I'm sure you are," she said softly, "but I can't just sit and talk with... strangers."

She stepped back to slip around him but he moved with her, blocking her escape.

Smiling, he said, "If we sit and talk for a while and get to know each other, then we won't be strangers."

While she tried to think of some way to politely refute his logic, he reached out and touched her hand again. Alien, prickly sensations made her skin tingle. She stared at the contrast of his sun-kissed, bronze skin on her almost painfully alabaster-white hand, then cautiously met his eyes again.

As he looked down at his fingertips on the back of her hand, his eyes widened. To her relief—and regret—he took his hand away.

Still unable to catch her breath, she turned and started to walk away.

He followed her out of the cafeteria. "One Coffee..."

"No, thanks." She walked on.

Devraj's long strides easily matched her hurrying gait.

No matter how cute Dev or Devraj was, non-Jewish was out of bounds.

And don't you forget it, Leah Abraham, as her grandmother would say in Russian. She straightened up, her resolution strengthening her nearly lost backbone.

Devraj was different from the other young men who'd approached her in the past weeks. None of them had gotten under her skin like this guy.

"I'm n-not one of your challenges."

"You don't know anything about me and you've judged me as some kind of... playboy. What if you're wrong?"

Just walk on. She was not a heroine living in a make-belief world, like in the novels and the movies she loved.

"You may be pleasantly surprised to find out I'm really a nice—and honest—guy. Come on, give me a chance." The urgent tone of his voice, so contradictory to his confident demeanor, made her footsteps falter, then stop.

Looking up at him, she didn't appreciate how he dwarfed her five-feet-seven height.

She stopped staring at his sculpted mouth. *So, he's good looking, so what? No interacting with boys, not even Jewish ones, without the elders' wise input.*

But why couldn't her grandparents treat her like a mature eighteen-year-old?

She'd see a kosher pig fly before that happened.

Her unfamiliar resentment frustrated her even more than this man's persistence.

She studied his stance, his obviously expensive clothes, and the casual way he wore the dark, butter-soft suede jacket she was tempted to touch. It grated on her how comfortable he seemed in the hustle bustle of the college atmosphere.

Her insides quaked, exhilarated yet terrified of being the object of this guy's attention. "I—I'm not your type." She marched on, picking up speed.

"What *is* my type?"

"I-I don't want to know." She continued walking.

"I'm very picky about my women." He was beside her again. "When I look at you, I like what I see. You're beautiful, smart and if you let me see your work, I'm sure I'd see just how talented you are."

She hated feeling this scared and out of her depth. He was probably challenged by her rejections, and would say fresh sweet-nothings to the next girl, as soon as Lia was out of earshot.

Nothing personal.

She stopped near the door of her next class, took in a deep breath, and let it out again. She faced him but refused to look into his hypnotic eyes. "Look, sorry to disappoint, but you're really not *my* type."

"What's not to like?" He grinned again, folding his muscular arms against a broad chest, accentuating the proud torso and forearm muscles through the jacket.

"You're very sure of yourself, m-must be nice."

He leaned against the wall, appreciation shining in his eyes. The corners of his well-defined mouth lifted, bringing out the most delicious dimples in his cheeks.

Even though she was shaking inside, another alien part of her wanted to stay and play his game.

Leaning towards her, in a soft, low voice so it was almost a caress, he said, "I'd like to be your personal model."

Shivers whispered against her skin. Heat flooded up her neck and face. She'd have loved to capture his bone structure and glorious physique but imagining him semi-naked made her feel warm all over, almost faint.

"S-sorry, I'm extremely choosy about my... my subjects."

With Devraj's lazy laughter following her, she felt breathless and conspicuous as she entered her classroom.

Exhausted yet excited, why did she want to jump for joy? Because some handsome guy had made her feel like she mattered, that he found her fascinating?

He'd called her beautiful, smart....

Oh, wake up, Lia; this is how the silver-tongued Bollywood god gets the girls worshipping at his feet.

He'd obviously seen her as easy bait.

Rushing to his Accounting class, Dev grinned, intrigued by Lia's defensiveness. Her words said one thing, but those amazing eyes betrayed her intense interest.

He was used to girls who dressed and acted like her trendy, leggy friend, Ella.

The type his friend, Jim, gravitated towards and then found them lacking; flirty, spoilt, expecting to get anything they pointed at.

But the aloof artist with the glossy dark braid drew him. If she was trying to hide her gorgeous curves, she was failing; with the graceful line of her delicate neck, and with every ballet-like movement of her slim body, she was more striking and exotic than any Hollywood actress he could think of.

Dev wanted to get to know the angelic, shy artist whom he'd watched from afar for too long. He'd bring a smile, of even laughter, into those molten-chocolate-brown eyes. Those eyes that hinted at a larger-than-life spirit buried within.

And he *would* see her drawings, and soon.

Chapter Two

TOO MANY TIMES during her Art History lecture, Lia reeled herself back to reality to concentrate. Everything related to art, ancient or modern, fascinated her, but not today.

This only proved men were a distraction she couldn't afford. She sighed. Her grandparents may be old-fashioned, but they were wise. The guy was probably already busy with more willing prey.

But exiting her class, her heart somersaulted at seeing Devraj leaning against the wall, as though he hadn't moved.

Obviously, education wasn't a priority to him. After all the hard work she'd gone through, and Aunt Eliza's nagging and cajoling to convince her grandparents to let Lia attend college, she wasn't impressed with Devraj taking his freedom for granted.

She walked off in the opposite direction, feeling like the coward that she was.

Again, he was beside her almost instantly.

"Please. Leave. Me. Alone."

She wouldn't look his way, but Devraj's strong hand on her arm pulled her towards him. His exotic scent sent her senses into overdrive, making butterflies swirl within her stomach and rib cage. She pulled her arm out of his hand. "You can't t-touch me." Her eyes scoured the passers-by. What if someone recognized her?

"Look, Lia, I don't go around chasing girls." All amusement was wiped off his face...

"No, they chase *you*," she muttered.

He must have heard her because he said, "And I don't care. I plucked up the courage to speak to you or you'd always stay an illusion, an enigma. See? I even know what those words mean." He grinned. "If you look them up in the dictionary you'll find a picture of you with that exact thunderous expression."

He'd needed courage to come to her? She bit back the smile threatening to betray her.

"I had to see the exact shade of your dark eyes. They're like molten chocolate." The intensity of his expression, despite another flashing smile, melted something deep within her abdomen, making her hungry for... what she didn't know.

Frustration bubbled within. "I'm sorry if you're not used to being rejected."

"You see? Another assumption. What if I'm rejected all the time?"

"Right, and I'm Cleopatra." Where were these alien, feisty words coming from?

He laughed softly, "I thought your name's Lia."

Shivers whispered against her skin. She wasn't sure if it was due to how he made her name sound intriguing, or that he'd asked about her.

"Let's just talk. You can trust me, Lia."

She blinked and looked into his eyes. "You don't understand the concept of 'no', do you?" She couldn't believe she was actually saying these words to this guy, whose muscular denim-clad chest rose and fell more deeply under her scrutiny.

"No." The unrepentant light played in his mischievous eyes. When his chuckle turned into a deep laugh, the sound was too much for her.

In mere seconds, her relieved, soft laughter joined his; why had she been so silly and cowardly?

He cocked his head slightly toward her. "I knew you'd have a lovely laugh."

She wanted to say the same about his contagious sense of fun. Forcing herself to stop looking at his sensuous mouth, she ordered her body to obey her mind's half-hearted command to start on her hour's journey home, but he leaned closer.

It took all her strength not to step back.

He gave her another smile that probably had girls fainting at his feet. "Don't be afraid of me."

Was she that transparent? Her cheeks flamed. "I'm not afraid. We simply have nothing in common."

His smile fell away. "I believe we have lots in common and I'm not like any of those guys I see trying to get your attention. When you get to know me you'll realize I'm better and smarter than they are, and much better looking....." The light in his eyes danced as he raised a dark eyebrow.

She shook her head trying not to smile again.

A pretty redhead sauntering by, flicked her glossy mane, while another girl threw meaningful looks in his direction.

But Devraj continued studying Lia—and only Lia. She reminded herself to breathe.

"Give me a chance. One coffee. Right now." When she shook her head again and started to walk on, he followed suit and added, "Or a double date with your friend and mine."

"Are you crazy? I can't. Please," she stopped and took in another steadying breath. "We shouldn't be seen talking."

"Shouldn't be seen?" He leaned closer, his voice going lower. "Is someone watching you? Do you have a boyfriend? Or..." He grinned. "Did your family arrange your marriage to some appropriate groom when you were four?"

"Something like that."

He grinned again. "Which one, the boyfriend, or the arranged marriage?"

Looking away, she contemplated telling him about Howard, the Jewish doctor whose grandmother was scheming with hers, brewing a suitable match.

Tradition and religion ruled the Abraham household.

She blurted out, "My proper name is Leah, and I'm Jewish. You're not. That's all that matters." She wouldn't add that no one but her grandparents called her by her Hebrew name. Or about how hard her aunt had worked for them to let Lia change her name to the more modern name, when she'd turned fourteen. She should also tell him about their marriage plans for her...

"Makes no difference to me."

"It does to *me*."

Devraj's smile waned. "I knew you were too good to be true."

She couldn't hide her smile.

When his smile broadened, she became too conscious of her shapeless, dull clothes. She wished she owned something fashionable, and that she looked more like her best friend, Ella. That she wouldn't be a stuttering mess whenever a guy made her nervous.

Once again, she was too aware how this sexy man filled ordinary stonewashed jeans, how the open suede jacket accentuated his perfect physique. She stared at his Adams apple and strong jaw. Glancing up, she saw him scanning her face, waiting. A slow Michael Jackson ballad—something about the girl liking the way the boy stared—reverberated in the now almost abandoned hall.

Blushing again, Lia was tempted to push at him, to get out of the invisible magnetic hold he had over her. "Don't stare at me." She said breathily.

"I can't help it." Devraj said gently. "Ever since I saw you that first week, I've wanted to meet you."

She almost believed his words.

Like a love-struck heroine in a heart-wrenching Bollywood movie, Lia expected to hear a familiar romantic burst of song.

Something was shifting inside her and that wouldn't do.

No more Bollywood movies for her. Not wanting to worry her grandmother by being late, Lia approached the exit doors.

"Look, Lia, I'm from a Hindu background, I know what it's like." His calm tone was persuasive as he walked beside her.

"If you really did, you'd leave me alone." She said softly.

"Oh, Lia, you know you like me. That's why you're fighting this..." He pointed to her and to himself. "And I don't agree with this old fashioned bull about traditions and culture any more than you do."

She shook her head. "You d-don't know what I believe."

She lowered her face, again resenting her grandparents describing her as shy and modest, as if they were compliments. Having always been a non-confrontational girl, Devraj brought out an alien part of her, making her want to stop living vicariously through her sassy, blonde friend and even her feisty Aunt Eliza. To taste real life.

Devraj's riling up your defense mechanism, that's all.

Turning away from him, she opened the exit door. She was glad to have a gust of nippy October air cool her face and neck, before she tightened her coat collar.

Devraj's words followed, "There's magic between us, Lia. It's as if... we're destined for each other. If it takes me forever, I'll prove it. You do believe in destiny, don't you?"

Because she did, she continued her escape. But she couldn't help taking a sideways peek.

Devraj was still staring, and raising his deep voice, he added, "Think about me, Lia."

Exhilaration and jumbled emotions which she'd felt only when she read romance novels, now made her want to believe this person.

Oh, boy, was he persistent, and so fun and so tempting!

Descending the stairs, she rushed away like Cinderella, suddenly sad leaving her prince behind forever.

Just one smile from Lia and Dev's world took on a fresh dimension. Underneath her insular shell, and that quiet angelic demeanor, he spied the lurking wit and sense of humor.

But he frowned at the damned sliver of guilt nagging him. Lia was right; he shouldn't be bothering her, imagining his sister in the same situation. To some degree, he understood why his parents had married off sweet Malika at eighteen.

But he wouldn't think about his own preplanned life in the mighty Shah dynasty, beneath the ostensible freedom. For the remaining academic year, he *was* his own man. When he was closer to his goal, he'd contemplate his next plans regarding architecture.

But right now, Lia challenged and inspired him to win her over. He'd get to know the elusive artist, earn her trust, and change her mind about him. And he would bring out that fiery spirit from within her.

Time. That was all he needed.

Maybe a little help, too. And he knew just whom to ask.

/ Chapter Three

THE MORE LIA learned, sketched, and painted, the more she realized how much she had yet to learn. The sense of imminent independence spurred her on. She focused on her goals, not letting anything or anyone distract her.

Even Devraj had got the message and left her alone for the past three days. She'd made sure she didn't sketch anything or anyone near *that* part of the cafeteria. But sometimes she suspected if she turned round she'd find him watching her.

She refused to make eye contact whenever she saw him. Art was a loner's paradise, her perfect companion. Men complicated everything. She'd never be like her Aunt Eliza, a thirty-six-year-old perpetual adolescent whose impulsive and eventful romantic adventures constantly resulted in heartbreak.

Later—much later—would she think about anything related to romance. She knew in her soul when the right time came she'd settle down, but never settle for second best. Right now, all that mattered was her art degree, which would be her ticket to freedom, to travel and teach in Europe. She sighed.

The old song, "Just an Illusion," followed her through the noisy hall into the cafeteria. Sitting at her usual spot in the corner, waiting for Ella, she fought the temptation to look at the table Devraj's group monopolized.

The familiar sensation of anticipation dampened her interest in her latest sketch. Annoyed by her distraction, she closed her pad. She was glad when Ella flung her violin case and music textbooks on the table and sat next to her.

Lia smiled at her friend. The two unlikely friends had clicked when they'd met at Aunt Eliza's office, two years ago, both working as junior assistants. Lia was the shy, ugly duckling with the risk of never becoming a swan, while Ella was a musical genius and rebel, thanks to her self-centered parents. It still amazed her how beneath that sophistication, the gorgeous, gifted Ella sometimes was so insecure about herself and her talents. They had their passion for art and their admiration for Aunt Eliza's business acumen in common.

They talked and caught up, giggling at Ella's latest sexy, social antics. Lia omitted mentioning Devraj. He wasn't bothering her, she reasoned, apart from sensing those vibes as if he was sending her telepathic messages—which *could* be her imagination—why jinx it?

"My grandmother invited you for Friday night dinner." Lia said.

"That sounds great." Ella said. "I love her cooking, even if I have to sit through their attempts to convert me to be a good girl." She chuckled. "Anyway, it's not as if I have a date. Oh, maybe I spoke too soon." Ella's eyes widened as if George Michael or Prince was coming towards her. Readying a dazzling smile, she drew her shoulders back to show off her perfect figure. "Look at that dishy bloke coming this way."

The tension in Lia's spine stung as she sat up straight.

"Hello again. Changed your mind yet, Lia?" The baritone voice was unmistakable.

Lia refused to acknowledge Devraj's presence or Ella staring at her. When she wouldn't respond to her friend's knee jab, Ella turned to Devraj with her flirtatious smile and said, "Hello, there."

Something unfamiliar coiled within Lia.

"Devraj's my name." Lia was tempted to add, *flirting is his game.*

"I'm Ella and you seem to know my friend—"

"We've met." He ignored Lia as he sat opposite her, his eyes fixed on Ella. That easy grin flashing perfectly white teeth told her he knew Ella would be ensnared by his charms.

"Really?" Ella looked about to burst with curiosity.

Lia stared at her closed pad again.

"But your friend's very reluctant to talk to me." Devraj said.

Lia stood up.

Fleetingly he glanced up at her, his eyes twinkling at Ella. "See what I mean? Can *you* ever have a long conversation with her?"

Lia pursed her lips, frustration boiling within her.

"I *am* working on her social skills."

Lia wouldn't look at the blonde, blue-eyed traitor who seemed just as interested in Devraj as he was in her.

"You're a good friend," he said.

"Lia's quite witty once you get to know her. But she's been acting strange—"

"Ella." Lia's voice sounded louder than she'd expected. Taking in a quick breath, she let it out, "I have to go." And before she realized it, she muttered, "I can't wait to find out which of his charming pick-up lines works on you."

Her friend's surprise shone brighter while Devraj smiled smugly, his raised eyebrow telling her, *Oops, your jealousy's showing.*

Eyes wide, Lia turned away and his laughter made her wish she had the guts to slap him. But what if instead of erasing that gleam in his eyes, he'd grab her and do something crazy like kiss her?

Where did that come from?

She glared at him over her shoulder, realizing she'd nearly rushed off without her stuff. As if knowing she'd rather eat live scorpions than risk touching him, his smirk stayed in place.

When he turned his charms back on Ella, Lia shoved the disturbing memory of how his touch had ignited something within her a mere seventy-two hours ago and she swiveled on her low heels and left the two alone.

Within minutes in the quiet of the women's restrooms, she admitted to her blushing reflection, she *was* jealous.

"The two-faced... Bloody good riddance to bad egoists!" she grumbled, taking in deep calming breaths, unfurling her fists.

Ella could handle him. They'd have beautiful children. Holding back tears Lia told herself not to be such a baby.

Lia needed peace, still feeling like a fool at scurrying away yesterday. She'd been unable to fall asleep until after one in the morning and now still groggy, staying away from the cafeteria, she was about to settle in a secluded corner of the library.

Breathing in the familiar reassuring scent of the studious atmosphere, she relaxed in the company of her second love, books.

Juggling her large bag with the sketchpad under one arm and two oversize art books and three novels in the other, Lia turned back from the book shelf she'd been perusing and bumped hard into a strong, warm wall.

Large, steadying hands grasped her by the forearms, as all her stuff, including her bag, scattered loudly by her feet.

Regaining her gravity her heart beat frantically as she felt sturdy arms against hers, moulding her towards a broad, warm chest. She recognized Devraj's divine scent of sandalwood intermingled with the sun just as his deep voice whispered into her right ear, "I've got you. You're safe." Having stopped her fall, now he'd probably think he was her hero.

"Let me go!" Her small voice came out muffled.

Had he followed her here? Lia hadn't seen Ella yet and didn't know what they'd talked about yesterday after she'd bolted. All evening last night she'd resisted picking up the phone 'to chat' with Ella. But even now, she squirmed inside at Devraj's gloating laughter.

Light headed, standing away from him, she saw the concern in his eyes turn into relief. The electric force between them made her vibrantly aware of the sounds and smells around her.

Widening the gap between them, she focused on calming herself.

Devraj crouched down to pick up her things, his eyes concentrating on her face as she kneeled beside him. She tried not to stare at his powerful thighs, those broad shoulders. Her face burned. What would she do for an encore? Head butt him?

Gathering up her remaining books, he smiled at her. "No 'thank you' for saving you just now? Didn't your parents teach—"

"They died when I was two."

His features straightened into a pained expression. "I'm so sorry. I shouldn't take things like that for granted."

"I-I'm sorry. I shouldn't have..." She almost whispered, her lips trembling. "Thanks."

Devraj stilled, staring at a sketch in his hand. Helpless, she saw him scan the curves she'd captured of him in the privacy of her bedroom. Sleep hadn't been her friend lately, as she relived the moments they'd exchanged earlier this week. She couldn't let him into her tiny, escapist world.

But she seemed to have no choice.

"Wow." He slowly breathed out the word, not raising his eyes from her work.

Pride swelling, her fear overwhelmed her.

He picked up another, glancing at her, then down at her drawings again.

Her pulse was erratic studying him as closely as he studied her work. Was she so starved for compliments she was hanging on every nuance on this stranger's face?

She rose from her knees. Gathering the handful of her remaining sketches and the large pad, he stood up too. "Is this how you see me, Lia?"

Attempting to take her work back, she watched his fingers hold on to it. She let go. Anchoring her treacherously wobbly limbs, she added, "P-please may I have those? It's just art." She couldn't help sounding defensive.

"You're good. This expression, it's as if you knew I felt ... caged." The vulnerability and new light of respect for her shone in his eyes.

Afraid that once again, a Bollywood movie track would play in the background, or at least in her mind, without looking at him Lia held out her free hand. "My sketches, please?"

As he returned her pad, she struggled to balance her stuff in her arms. With one step he took her load from her. After a moment's relief, the emptiness in her arms left her feeling more vulnerable.

He took the few steps towards her favourite nook she'd planned to settle in, and put down her stuff.

"Thanks..." She said grudgingly. "I have lots of studying to do, so if you don't mind..."

"There's plenty of space; I can study alongside you."

Had her skepticism shown? A corner of his mouth lifted, "I do study, you know."

At her squirming shrug, he added, "I won't distract you. I

want the same thing you do."

"What?" Was she blushing again?

"I need peace and quiet, and you have this serene demeanour—I like having calm people around me."

More heat blazed in her face and neck. "But I don't want company."

"I noticed. The only person you hang out with is Ella. You've got a nice friend."

So why are you here, and not with her?

She sat at the table in the suddenly too-intimate space.

"What about boys as friends?" He asked as he sat next to her. When she looked at him, he held out his free hand in a gesture of peace. "OK, your expression tells me you don't believe men and women can be friends."

"No, I told you already." She sighed, turning slightly away from him in her seat.

"What about the culture differences? That's really old-fashioned, don't you think?"

"It took so much to get my grandparents to let me attend college, you'd never understand it. Now, please, before we're seen together, please leave."

Beyond him, she glanced at the studious groups scattered around the quiet space, a few feet away from them.

All she needed was someone from her community, like Uri, the rotund neighbourhood gossip's son to see her and for the news of her talking intimately with any boy, to get back to her grandparents.

"Look, let's get to know each other and if I ever even touch you or make you feel uncomfortable, or if I even enter your personal space, you can slap me and walk away."

The mischief shining in his eyes made her bite her lower lip. "You mean invading my personal space, like you are right now?"

He moved his chair a tiny inch away from hers.

She smiled despite the feeling of doom and stepping on unfamiliar quicksand-like territory. Devraj was chili hot and just as dangerous, especially as she was deadly allergic to any kind of chili peppers.

Yet Lia lingered and wanted him to stay, too.

As if aware of her change of mind Devraj asked, "So, how about a double date tomorrow night? Our friends seem to be intrigued with each other."

Was that why he'd spoken to Ella? Her relieved heart fluttered as she shook her head. "No."

She looked around her again in case her panicky voice had attracted attention. "E-Ella wouldn't go for your friend, who..." She couldn't seem to find the right words.

Devraj grinned, "Who goes through girls faster than disposable plates at a party." Then shrugged, "Jim's not all bad, and he broke up with the girl he was with. I just thought you'd prefer to be chaperoned."

She frowned, keeping her shaking fingers clasped on her lap. If he knew she was so afraid, why was he even here? "No."

"All I want is to get to know you, Lia. Just think about it— one dinner date. After that, you don't have to see me again. Now let's start over." He smiled that grin again. "I'm Devraj Shah, but you can call me David or Dev if you'd prefer."

"Devraj Shah." She tried it on her tongue.

"I like the way you say it. Only my parents call me that, but suddenly I like it much more. It means King of Gods, but I'd have preferred King of Love."

Her nerves made her giggle but then she stopped herself.

"And you *can* trust me, Lia." The grin disappeared and the seriousness in Devraj's expression intensified, making her insides quiver.

Without words, that hypnotic haze pulled her to him again, and felt the back of his fingers softly stroke her cheek.

Gasping, her breath became more erratic, her knees no sturdier than liquid honey. Thank goodness she was still sitting. As if under the same spell, he leaned closer. Much too close, but she couldn't move. Her heart revving into overdrive, she gazed at him. Was he going to kiss her or something?

Pulling away, she resisted touching the burning skin where he'd left his warmth. No one had ever caressed her like this. Needing to break the trance she pushed at him and felt his chest muscles pulse under her touch and instantly recoiled, heat enveloping her body.

Feeling like a marshmallow about to be roasted, she forced her wobbly limbs to let her stand up and as he watched, she gathered her belongings and rushed away towards the library doors.

Before she reached them, Devraj gripped the handle, holding it momentarily, as if determined to keep her there.

Then he opened it and let her go through. "Miss me, Lia. I hope you change your mind about the date and we see each other tomorrow."

Chapter Four

"SO, LET'S DO it, Lia, it'll be fun." Ella said as she drove down Stamford Hill to Lia's grandparents for Friday night dinner.

"I don't think so—"

"Don't play games, Lia, I know you want to. You're scared stiff because you're so attracted to Devraj. But he's only a guy, for Pete's sake."

Shaking inside, Lia stayed quiet.

"It's only a double date; taste some freedom for a change. I'll take care of you."

Turning on the left indicator, Ella manoeuvred her Golf into Lia's road. "So, should we do it?"

"You just want to go out with that Jim." Lia said.

"I can go out with him without chaperoning you, so don't avoid my question."

"Even if I wanted to, I know my grandparents won't let me."

"You know you can convince them to let you sleep over at my place for one measly night. But so you don't sabotage it, leave them to me. I told Devraj I'd call him in the morning if we're on for tomorrow night. So if you're allowed to come, you'll do it, right?" She parked the car and grinned at Lia.

"N-no!"

"You know you want to, and I'll make it happen."

Lia didn't like the expression on her friend's face as they entered the house. Although she wouldn't admit it, a frisson of excitement tingled up and down her spine.

What could be the harm in a double date to see how real people lived?

Lia watched her family sitting around the food-laden kitchen table; the subdued Aunt Eliza and Baboola looked tired and tight-lipped. Again, they'd probably argued about her aunt's latest unsuitable boyfriend. Dedda looked tired and preoccupied since he'd returned from synagogue.

Lia couldn't summon up an appetite for *plov,* her favorite chicken and rice dish.

Her heart beat frantically as she exchanged glances with Ella, who cleared her throat delicately, and put down her fork. "So, Mr. and Mrs. Abraham, is it OK for Lia to come over tomorrow afternoon and help me study? She's the only one who can help me. Then we can catch a movie and I can drop her off home at around eleven?"

Her aunt looked pointedly at her mother. Baboola seemed to study the three women in turn.

Dedda, oblivious to any tension, now studied his wife, his salt and pepper bushy eyebrows furrowed over his hooded eyes.

Lia held her breath. After an eternity, Baboola said in her slow, heavily accented English, "Our Leah is becoming independent. You're such a blessing to us, Leah, our angel. You can sleep at Ella's mother's flat if you want."

Lia's guilt was stomped by her excitement and instant fear of the impending freedom. She'd never slept over anywhere but at her aunt's place.

"At last." Aunt Eliza mumbled, but Baboola seemed to ignore her words. Mother and daughter exchanged a look of temporary truce. Lia suspected her aunt had once again been lobbying for her niece's freedom.

"That would be great, wouldn't it, Lia?" Ella smiled casually, while her eyes betrayed her sense of accomplishment.

"Are you sure you'll manage with everything until Sunday?" Lia asked and felt a sharp kick in her shin.

Ella stared at Lia as Baboola answered. "Yes, after Shabbat I'm seeing Rena and picking up the alterations for Mrs. Levinson. They'll keep me busy for most of Sunday. So you have a nice time, girls."

Still stunned, Lia swallowed hard.

"I know I can trust our Leah, and you're a good girl under those..." Baboola looked at Ella and then back at Lia. In Russian she asked, "How do you say, daring clothes?"

Lia translated and Ella smiled, "Yes, we're good girls and you know you and Lia are a good influence on me."

Dedda watched and said nothing, although he understood English. Surrounded by other Russian Jewish families in the close-knit community and even at work—overlaying the wood panels inside the Rolls Royce cars he loved—Dedda still managed to get by without speaking much English.

As Lia got up and started clearing the dirty plates and cutlery, she realized she'd tuned out the conversation at the table for a few moments.

As she returned to the table, she heard Baboola say, "That's why it's so important to choose the right Jewish man to marry in the first place."

Lia noticed Baboola steal a glance at Aunt Eliza. But both her aunt's ex-husbands had been Jewish. They still hadn't been good enough. Her grandmother's glare shifted to Dedda who sipped his small, gold-rimmed cup of green tea. Like a ritual, he held the dainty cup in his delicate, wrinkled hands with fingers of a master of his trade.

Becoming attuned to the tension in the woman he'd shared most of his life with, Dedda lifted his wise eyes and studied Aunt Eliza. When he looked back at Baboola, she waved a slow hand, as if to say, "later." After almost fifty years together, Lia knew how easily they communicated without words.

"Leah, my angel," Baboola suddenly had an excited edge to her voice. "Rena asked when you'll meet Howard again."

Even though said in Russian, Lia flushed, and said, "I've only spoken to her grandson for a few minutes and I don't want to be rude, but I told you I'm not ready for any commitment yet." She avoided Ella's stare from across the table.

"Howard's a very nice, charming man," Baboola said. "He's a brilliant surgeon, and at such a young age. His family is Ashkenazi and they've been in UK for the past three generations. He keeps asking when you can meet."

"Let's talk about that later, Baboola." Lia got up. "Thank you for dinner."

"Yes, thank you so much." Ella chimed in.

"Is there anything else we can do to help?" As if understanding Lia's impatience to leave, both her aunt and Baboola waved the girls out of the kitchen.

Once they escaped into the quiet of Lia's room, she sagged against the door.

Ella began to giggle while Lia begged her to be quiet.

"That went better than I'd hoped." Ella said with an air of 'another job well done.' "And tomorrow I'll get to work on your eyebrows and everything." Her friend rubbed her hands, staring at Lia's hair and face, as if imagining this Cinderella already transformed. "But right now, you'll tell me all about this Howard."

Chapter Five

LIA ASKED HERSELF how Ella had talked her into this crazy scheme as she tried to sit still, suffering through the makeover. Ella plucked another one of Lia's agonizingly thick eyebrow hairs.

Her friend smiled like a Cheshire cat who'd swallowed the fairy godmother and her wand.

As Lia held her breath again, Ella said, "Breathe, Lia. I'm doing a good deed for humanity. Now people will notice your gorgeous features, those beautiful eyes, instead of the Frieda unibrow."

"I never had a unibrow, Barbie Perfect! Ouch," Lia groaned again. "But if we hadn't met at Aunt Eliza's office we wouldn't be this close and you wouldn't be torturing me right now." Lia held her breath again.

Ella giggled. "I remember how jealous you were thinking I'd steal her affection from you."

Lia had envied Ella's connection with Aunt Eliza over music

and their gutsy sense of fun. Her aunt had always wanted to become a pianist, but had never been able to make the leap. Whenever Lia heard her speak with Ella about their passion, she understood why her aunt was such an empathetic advocate for Lia's artistic endeavours. But the only thing that had alleviated her jealousy was when the astute Aunt Eliza had hugged her and told her, "You're like my own baby, Lia. You'll always be my special baby. I really like Ella but I love and adore *you*!"

Now she focused on her friend saying, "We're great together, I bring you out into the real world and you keep me grounded. Right, Lia?"

As she finished, Ella stood back, admired her work and wrapped her arms around Lia.

She hugged her friend back, but her smile turned into mortification when she saw her reflection in the mirror. She gaped at the ridiculously tight hot pink boob tube Ella had insisted on, and felt like a half-dressed pole-dancer about to go on stage.

At least she'd won the battle over wearing the tiny black thing Ella had called a mini-skirt. Yet, she couldn't believe how revealing the figure-hugging jeans were on her suddenly long legs. Her makeup was perfect, admittedly, although her eyes didn't look the same. They looked bigger, more mature.

When had her body grown these breasts and curves? She determined the black jacket would stay on even if she had to sew it on around herself.

Her mouth felt dry thinking of facing Devraj. He was used

to sophisticated, worldly girls. She hadn't even left London for vacations or started taking driving lessons yet. She was way too nervous to contemplate yet another hurdle she'd have to get over with her grandparents. Her breath shuddered out of her.

"What?"

"What am I going to talk about, El? Not only do you know so much about music, but you've visited so many exotic places and I feel like the village idiot wrapped in country bumpkin." Was she going to have a panic attack?

Ella giggled again, shaking her head. "Just be yourself. You're interesting and witty when you don't clam up. They're just blokes, remember."

What had possessed her to start the ball of lies rolling at home? Before she could change her mind, Ella whisked her out of the flat.

As Ella's Golf convertible neared the restaurant Ella and Devraj had chosen for the double date in the centre of London, and let the valet park their car, Lia's insides felt wobbly. Her shoes felt like stilts as she followed Ella, whose hips wiggled as if she was born in those heels.

She ought to be grateful her first date was going to be supervised, but the nagging guilt of having lied to her grandparents stuck in her throat—or was it the anticipation of seeing Devraj again?

Would he think she'd tried to impress him?

What if she was sick all over him? She took in deep breaths and jumped when Ella squealed, "There they are, right on time." Ella waved and her bangles on her wrist made exciting music. Her sexy little black and silver dress showed off her low cleavage and curves perfectly.

Lia's heart thudded as they approached the two handsome men waiting outside the restaurant in the clear, cool night. She could lock herself in the ladies' room, she thought, focusing on looking calm.

As Devraj wasn't Jewish, nothing would come of this evening. She imagined him yawning at her statue-like presence. It was for the best; he'd see there was nothing interesting or unique about her. She need never see him again, be jumpy, or have to lie to her grandparents.

Soothed by a millionth of a fraction, she let her jelly-like legs carry her to the smiling guys. She swallowed a groupie-like sigh at seeing the relaxed Devraj.

He studied her appreciatively, his surprise turning into amusement.

As they waited for their table in the bustling atmosphere of the dimly lit Italian restaurant, Ella reeled Jim into their own conversation. Jim listened and nodded with an almost indulgent smile on his handsome face. His green eyes were even more intense at such close proximity, but Lia was only affected by Devraj's physical pull beside her, feeling him watching her.

"Ella's clothes and Ella's make up." She said.

"You look lovely. Are those shoes comfortable?" he grinned.

He'd picked up her discomfort, although she was enjoying being only a few inches shorter than him now. She blushed, trying not to stutter, "It's unfortunate Ella and I are the same size. I'd have preferred my flats, but she insisted on being my fairy godmother." Did she sound like a nervous idiot?

"Cinderella pales in comparison." He touched her waist, sending tingles through her body. Discreetly, his hand on the small of her back, supported her careful gait as they followed the chattering Ella and quiet Jim to their table.

Sliding into the intimate corner booth, padded with deep-plum leather seats, they opened their heavy, burgundy menus and Lia's panic welled up. The last time she'd eaten out was with her Aunt Eliza at Garfunkels six months ago. She didn't go out much, because her grandparents preferred to stay at home. To say she felt out of her depth was like saying the arctic was slightly cold.

Sitting beside her Devraj smelled divine and looked virile with the top button of his cream shirt open under the soft black leather jacket. She studied the menu, but the words swam in her vision. Were they in hieroglyphics? Devraj's warmth so close to her made her aware of how her erratic breathing made her chest rise and fall. Closing her menu with clammy hands, she peeked at Devraj from the corner of her eye, and then watched Ella sitting across from her.

But her friend was oblivious to her.

As the rest of them threw around their ideas of starters and main courses, Lia sank in her seat. What was she doing here?

They shut their menus and Ella aimed her most winning smile at Jim. Lia peeked at her date again. She couldn't believe she was actually out with Devraj.

Concentrating on what Ella was saying she only heard, "my parents' divorce taught me never to get serious about anything until I'm established in my career."

"Clever girl." The reserved Jim smiled. Was that relief or mutual respect blooming between him and Ella?

When the waiter came to take their order, Lia stiffened, wishing she could hide like a turtle in her shell. She'd been so busy soaking up the atmosphere and listening to everyone else, she'd forgotten about food.

As her companions ordered exotic sounding Italian dishes Lia had never heard of, her breathing became more constrained.

"And you?" Everyone watched her.

Her face warm, feeling faint, she heard Devraj say, "I think the lady will share my house salad and what about the vegetarian lasagna?"

Staring into his eyes, gratitude as huge as Niagara Falls washed over her. She nodded and her lips formed the tiniest smile.

As the waiter left them, and Jim and Ella carried on their own conversation, Devraj said, "You're lucky to be doing what you're passionate about. You're very talented."

"Thank you." Again, she sounded quiet among the throng of diners and the elegant, jovial atmosphere. The rich, new, mouth-watering scents of plates of food passing by them mingled with fragrant coffee and cinnamon, made Lia determined to start trying more new experiences.

She looked at Devraj, "You're probably used to girls who are more... talkative."

"It's refreshing to be with someone who doesn't need to be

entertaining every second." His voice lowered slightly. "It's nice just being with you, even if we're not alone." He touched her hand on her lap and with a jolt, she pulled her hand away. She reached out to pick up her water, but couldn't trust her trembling fingers.

Ella blinked at her, raising a perfect thin eyebrow. Lia ignored her, planning to kick her friend's behind for not dissuading her from going through with this date.

It would be too intimate to share the same plate, she thought, staring at the salad placed between her and Devraj. As if aware of her fears, he served a few forkfuls of the crisp tangy-smelling leaves onto her side plate. Again, he glanced at her as Ella described the many shows she'd seen and the many places her parents had taken her to—separately—over the years.

Lia yearned she could learn to be within her element in situations Ella took for granted. But here she was, out on a double date for the first time.

As she started enjoying a second spoonful of the delicious lasagna, Jim asked, "So I hear you were born in Russia. How old were you when you left?"

Lia swallowed the mouthful, reminding herself that she'd never see them again. Scrunching her napkin within her hands she said, "I was nearly three. Soon after my parents' death my grandparents decided to give my aunt and me a new life without the painful memories."

The silence at their table made her realize she may have divulged too much personal information instead of keeping it light and entertaining.

"Have you gone back to visit?" Devraj asked.

"I've wondered about the place where I was born, and the house I lived in, but I'd never say anything to my grandparents."

"Dev's gone to India to see his parents' birth place, haven't you? Aren't you planning to go there again soon?" There was amusement in Jim's green eyes.

Devraj watched him through narrowed eyes. "Yes, I've seen a lot of India."

"How I wish I could do that, and see all those places I've only read about or seen in Bollywood films..." She sounded like an over-enthusiastic child. She clamped her mouth shut, feeling heat rise up her neck and face.

"You watch Bollywood films?" Devraj smiled.

"I-I keep my aunt and grandmother company when *they* do."

"When Lia finishes her art degree," Ella rolled her fork in her succulent looking shrimp pasta, "she plans to explore the world, starting with teaching art in Europe."

"Where else have you travelled to already?" Devraj asked.

Lia gulped, "Nowhere, yet."

"Make sure you stay true to your goals." Jim said. "Life has a way of changing your plans while you're looking elsewhere."

"As you can hear, my friend's rather philosophical even after just one beer."

"That's very mature of a guy who's just...What? Twenty, twenty-one?" Ella asked.

"Dev and I are both twenty, he skipped two school years, I just skipped one."

Devraj shrugged and shifted slightly beside Lia. "Suppose, it's meant to be."

"Ah, another one who believes in destiny." Ella smiled at her. "Lia believes we each have our destinies mapped out for us. I just learned from her grandparents that in the Jewish religion, the baby's destiny is preordained forty days before it's even conceived."

Lia felt Devraj's eyes on her but wouldn't glance his way. She tried not to sound defensive as she said, "That's what our culture believes."

"You believe in destiny." He looked rather pleased with himself when she glanced sideways at him. "So, is exploring the world part of your destiny, Lia?" Devraj asked.

Something happened to her insides every time he said her name. It made her sound gloriously interesting, unique. She broke eye contact. "I hope it is. I plan to work hard towards the plan and see—"

"Unfortunately Lia's grandparents have other plans for her." Was Ella going to mention the archaic matchmaking and Howard? "They keep her quite close to home, and she'd been to an all girls' school till last year, can you imagine that?"

Lia slowly released her held breath.

Jim grinned, "I wouldn't mind going to an all girls' school." He raised his eyebrows and his smile broadened when Ella playfully thumped his thick arm.

Lia flinched. Would she ever be able to breathe normally in the company of the opposite sex?

"So do *you* believe in destiny, Jimmy?" Ella asked, fluttering her long eyelashes. The sexual charge between them made Lia feel like a voyeur.

"I strongly believe each of us is in charge of our future, our own destiny." Jim said.

Ella beamed at him and threw her arms around his neck. "That's exactly what I think."

Appearing un-phased by her show of affection, Jim smiled as if indulging a child.

"That's an oxymoron, isn't it?" Devraj said, then added, "Destiny is something we can't change, only our decisions can change our future."

"You know all about that, don't you, Dev? About family obligations and how some people's destinies are all planned out by birth order or just because they're male." Jim grinned good-naturedly.

From the corner of her eye, Lia saw Devraj shooting him a warning look. "That's right, Fred. Or Guinness." Devraj's lips twitched slightly at Jim's obvious dislike of his nicknames.

Ella laughed softly. "I can see where you got 'Fred' from, his adorable freckles and red hair, but couldn't you have come up with a more original nickname than Guinness?"

"But Guinness isn't Jim's choice of drink. He's called that after he got into the Guinness Book of Records."

This time Jim flashed an undisguised warning look at his friend.

"Really? How?" Ella moved closer to Jim.

Devraj grinned. "As he's too modest, I'll tell you. At the age of three he was the youngest boy who could play any tune he heard on the piano."

"Oh, it's like having a photographic memory but for music." Ella cooed touching his arm. "You lucky guy. I wish I had that gift. So will you be competing at next week's contest?"

"No. I don't play much these days." Jim shrugged as if they were discussing the weather. "I help out with the fund raisers in my own way." Ella grilled him about the details of his gift. He answered her questions as if bored. As Ella smoothed a strand of Jim's hair from his temple, Lia watched, mesmerized. Would she ever be able to feel that free to express her own emotions and go after whatever she wanted?

She'd have loved to ask more about Devraj, but her tongue seemed glued to the roof of her mouth.

Lia was a disgrace to womankind. She vowed never to stay quiet and subservient in any parts of her life.

How she was going to accomplish that was another matter. Knowing what she wanted wasn't enough. But she'd find a way to etch true freedom, and really live, travel, and enjoy every minute; without worrying about making mistakes and hurting anyone, especially her grandparents.

But right now, she wanted to survive this double date and rush back to the safety of Ella's flat.

Lia was afraid she'd cry. How could Ella have invited Jim and Devraj back to her place? According to her friend, it was too early in the evening to call it a night after the long walk down the Embankment. Lia had refused to 'keep Devraj company' in his car on the short journey back to Ella's flat, and when she had her alone in the Golf, Lia's panicky words fell on deaf ears. She'd grinned when Lia had wanted her to take her back to her grandparents. "Yes, they'd be ecstatic to see you and your new wardrobe."

Now Lia stood alone with Devraj in the kitchen, listening to her friend giggling in the cozy living area, a few feet away.

She shivered as delicious waves of fear and exhilaration sent goose bumps at being so close to Devraj.

"Are you cold? Here—" Devraj started to take off his jacket. It wasn't cold in the flat.

She stopped him by touching his forearm. She moved away from his warmth as if he was radioactive. As if emboldened by her physical proximity, he neared her.

She jumped away again. "Please. I have to go, I can't stay." Although she couldn't interrupt the escalating physical attraction between their friends, she was afraid he'd offer to give her a lift. "I'll call my aunt to pick me up. I'm sorry I'm such a bore."

"You don't think I was expecting—anything like *that*?" Devraj pointed a thumb towards the living area, frowning.

Her inexperience prickled, weighing her down.

He looked offended, even disappointed. "You don't have to go, I'll get Jim out of here in two minutes."

The relief made her want to buckle down onto the kitchen counter. "Ella won't be happy," she breathed out.

"Leave them to me." Before turning away fully, he looked at her. "I enjoyed this evening, very much."

From his intimate expression, she feared he'd come nearer

and kiss her, but he hesitated for only a fraction before leaving her alone.

She heard Ella's laughter subside, then sporadic words like, "That's a great idea," from Ella and "Why not?" from Jim.

Soon Ella led the guys to the kitchen with a satisfied smile. "Devraj suggested we all have lunch near Tower Bridge tomorrow. What do you think?"

No way. "I'm expected back home by lunchtime, I'm sorry. But you go ahead."

"What if we start early and we drop you off just after lunch?" Ella's eyes begged.

"I'll bring my camera, it may be an inspiring couple of hours for the artist and the architect in us?" Devraj added, again standing close to her.

How could she be ungrateful after he was keeping his promise to leave so soon? Compromises were a part of life.

Obviously taking her hesitation as agreement, Devraj smiled and offered his hand. "See you tomorrow, Rani."

Lia blushed. He'd called her 'queen' in Hindi.

"What's Rani?" Ella asked.

"I'll tell you tomorrow." Devraj said, holding Lia's hand. When had she given it?

"*Ciao.*" He let her hand go as if hesitant to leave.

Why was she looking forward to seeing him again? Because, she reasoned, he was smart and fun.

So much for will power.

Chapter Six

SUNDAY WAS A cold but gorgeously bright day. Almost immediately, Ella and Jim went off on their own, strolling by the bank under the looming Tower Bridge. Alone with Devraj again, Lia was glad she'd brought her sketchbook, as inspiration could strike anywhere, especially with the weather being so gracious for this time of year.

The company was exciting yet surprisingly calming in the cool afternoon breeze.

She was distracted by how the meticulous Devraj settled almost reverently on a shot before capturing certain angles of the sunlit bridge with his expensive-looking camera. His attention seemed fully focused on the regal construction until she happened to look up from her drawing and catch him watching her. Had he taken a photo of her without her knowing?

From afar, Lia caught the flirtatious Ella nuzzle into Jim as they meandered farther away, by the grassy edge of the sparkling Thames river. The growing sparks between them made her hope Ella could protect herself from being hurt.

Settling beside her on the bench, Devraj asked her about their favorite books and films.

Refusing to sound like a soppy romantic, especially after he'd smiled, raising an eyebrow at her choice of novels at the library on Friday, she wouldn't mention enjoying watching Bollywood movies or that she enjoyed listening to the classic singers Mohammed Rafi and Lata Mangeshkar. Instead, she mentioned her other favorites: Michael Jackson, George Michael, Elvis, and any music from the late 1950s and the 60s.

He loved Jazz and R&B and he played the acoustic guitar.

She found out they had in common the love of science fiction films, like the classic 'The Terminator.' She didn't divulge that it was because of its poignant love story. They also talked about the 'Raiders of the Lost Ark' film.

She noted his wistful expression, when he mentioned the old movie, 'Field of Dreams.' If he believed in Kevin Costner's vision of "if you build it they will come," she hoped he'd achieve his own dreams.

"My older brother, Rav, and my father would have liked me to join the family business, but…" He looked away, "maybe we *can* control our future."

The bond within his family was unmistakable as he elaborated on his brother's life, and his new bride who'd come from India five years earlier. "They're still trying for a baby and it hasn't happened yet."

He talked about his sister Malika, her husband Ajay and

their little boy Sanjay. When he showed a picture of his nephew, the boy was so sweet and had an uncanny resemblance to Devraj.

She smiled at the brightness in his eyes when he spoke of his softhearted mother. After a moment of silence, he asked softly, "I don't suppose you remember anything but what your grandparents have told you about your parents."

Before she realized it, she was telling him about the taboo subject, her parents' death. When Lia was two years old, her father was returning from the nearest city, and had run a red light rushing to get to her mother who was in hospital with a ruptured appendix. "It was the middle of the night, still snowing heavily. They died minutes apart." She stared unseeing at the blue sky reflected in the Thames.

"I can't imagine losing...," Devraj said tightly, swallowing. "Your poor family."

Blinking, Lia was touched at his tender expression.

"I can't believe I'm talking about the past, on a beautiful day like this." She tried to shake off her melancholy, bringing her raincoat closer around herself.

"I'm glad you trust me." Then he changed the subject.

Just being with Lia, enjoying their interactions and getting to know her, made Dev question his years in university. Damn, he questioned his whole life—which was suddenly too predictable and staid. Sure, he had fun and friends, and his studies kept him stimulated enough, but Lia's quiet passion for art made him impatient to start his own life, instead of swimming down river of his preplanned family destiny under the ostensible freedom. Simply being with her made him believe in infinite possibilities. Architecture sang in his veins as strongly as art was Lia's calling.

They'd become good friends, if not much more.

Every time her shy smile reached the depths of her dark eyes, he wanted to touch her, but refrained. He wanted to see that smile shining in her eyes again. Nothing but architecture inspired him as much as Lia did.

His future, freedom, and adventure beckoned.

"I like that passion in you." He pointed at her sketchpad. "May I?" His fingers were poised over the larger sketchpad that hadn't shed its load in the library.

Hesitation and something else warred within her eyes as he waited.

Relaxing her shoulders, she shrugged.

Slowly opening the art pad, a frisson of excitement rippled through him at the honour.

And there, on the first page, he saw the sign.

Chapter Seven

LIA'S HEARTBEAT DRUMMED too fast. This sketchpad held her drawings and studies of her most prized Seven Wonders of the World subjects, among others.

Studying the page, Devraj almost breathed out the words, "The Taj Mahal."

The pure appreciation, which no actor could emulate, brought goose bumps to her skin. When he looked into her eyes, she was afraid he'd see into her soul.

"You're really good." He said simply. "You've captured its magic and the perfect architecture so well. So why the Taj Mahal?" The rising and falling of his chest seemed more prominent as he studied it and then stared at her.

She blushed, clasping her hands on her knees.

"Isn't it like a sign?"

"I d-don't believe in signs." *Liar, Liar, your beetroot-red face on fire!* "The Taj Mahal's one of the Seven Wonders of the World, that's all." She stammered. "I also love the Sphinx and the Pyramids, Niagara Falls, the Grand Canyon—"

"But none of them match the beauty of the Taj Mahal." His eyes challenged her. "Or have that legacy of love."

She never tired of painting it. "I'll go there one day." It was her number one dream to explore and paint in India. "Have *you* visited the Taj Mahal, or do only tourists do that?" Did she sound like an over-enthusiastic groupie for all things Indian?

"A few times. It's quite magical. The white marble of the huge building, the inspired architecture, and the grounds are unique."

He leaned closer toward her. "Early studies show the original gardens had been more like a paradise, planted with roses, daffodils, and fruit trees? It was only when the British took over the management that they replaced all that with lawns. Sad, really. But my favorite's the intricate architecture. That's what I call inspired genius."

She nodded, and despite knowing the story, having studied some of it in class, she was newly fascinated by his enthusiasm as he talked about the deep meaning and the strong love story embroiled in the palace and the fifth Mughal emperor. "In 1631 the Shah Jahan built the monument to declare his love to his second wife, Mumtaz Mahal. 'Taj Mahal' means the Crown Palace. Did you know it took over forty years to complete?"

She nodded again and found herself relaxing, smiling.

He talked about the amount of marble and precious gems used in the detailed work all over the palace.

She understood his passion so well. "You make me want to go there even more. So you're studying architecture?" She regretted the question at his disappointed expression.

He shook his head. "No." He turned the page to her next drawing of a detailed angle of the marble interior. "I'm doing my MBA in Accounting and Economics. I'm taking architecture next year." He paused for a moment then added, "That's the deal, although I know my father would have still liked me to join the family business. Shah Imports is an importer of fine goods."

The detachment wasn't lost on her.

"I'm glad my older brother enjoys working with my father and uncle. But... I feel sorry for him." He looked like he'd never uttered this aloud. "He's twenty-five and his career and life were laid out for him since he knew how to add and subtract at three years old."

"Well, I'm happy that you'll get a chance to study your passion. I can't imagine doing anything but art." She found herself adding, "if it hadn't been for my aunt, my grandparents would never have given me permission."

"I'm so glad they did." That warm look made her skin tingle again.

Her pulse raced erratically as she watched him turn to the next sketch of the latter pages of her pad. She feared she'd feel too exposed at his perusal of her intimate life drawings.

Instead, he made her feel like it was the most natural thing to capture the miracle and imperfection of male and female anatomy. Afraid of people laughing or making lewd comments, she only shared her pieces with her aunt and Ella.

Devraj seemed to appreciate the work for what it was. Art.

"What does your family think about these?" He studied her as if seeing something other people didn't notice in her or her work.

"My Aunt Eliza raves about my talents. My grandparents... would freak." An understatement of the century. She bit her lower lip. "They'd probably call in the Rabbi to exorcise the evil out of me, like Ella likes to joke." She smiled.

"I like your passion, being so driven about your art. I almost envy it." She stared at his brooding expression. "I like you, Lia."

Her throat constricted and she couldn't speak.

"There are so many similarities between our cultures, I really know—" His tone was calm, persuasive, as if aware of the shift within her.

"Look, just because I let you see my work—"

"Why did you?"

Her shrug turned into a squirm.

"Because you know you can trust me. I'd never hurt you, Lia. But you could hurt *me*." He said. "Let's be friends, Lia." The way he pronounced the name, his velvety low voice made her want to be a grownup. A woman who knew what she wanted and went after it. A woman who enjoyed her power over men.

But that was not her. Was it?

She *wanted* to start living her own life.

"I don't know. Have you had platonic relationships with girls before?"

"Of course I have, when I was six."

She burst out laughing.

Devraj blinked and smiled. "I like making you laugh. You

look so happy and free. Please, don't be afraid of... us, Lia."

Something deep within her shifted. She'd had enough of feeling like a child refusing to share her toys.

Slowly blowing out a held breath, she let her shoulders come down a notch. What could be the harm in them having lunch sometimes? Everyone did it. He looked like the last person on earth to hurt her. The generous, fun-loving nature shone through him, making her feel special and interesting.

"You can trust me, Lia. Because," the pause made her stare at his mouth, "we both know you feel that special pull between us. As if we're destined lovers reincarnated from centuries ago. Hindus believe in reincarnation, like Jews, and that's just one of many similarities." His deep voice was soothing. Surrounded by his fresh scent, her mind shot out crazy questions, like what if she *was* fighting the inevitable?

Dev watched Lia's shoulders relax another notch.

Her silky skin looked satiny and tempting and her plump, naked lips made him hungry with curiosity. He detected the delicate apple and cinnamon scent emanating from her. Would her rich, dark brown hair feel super soft between his fingers?

When Lia's gaze seemed lost in the sunny vista of the bridge on the Thames, Dev suddenly wondered if she was hiding something.

Seeing Jim and Ella slowly making their way back towards them, he faced Lia. "Don't let your talents go to waste."

She stared in that adorable way, as if wondering whether she should trust him.

"I'll help you stick to your dream, if you help me, too. Deal?"

Offering her his hand, he asked, "Friends?"

After a fraction of hesitation, she smiled and shook his hand.

Chapter Eight

"BE A GOOD girl, now." Ella smiled, as Lia exited the car outside her grandparents' house at two that afternoon.

As if walking on a cloud, she let herself quietly into the dim, narrow hallway, gently closing the door. She felt naughty as if guilt and the remaining euphoria of the hours spent with Devraj were painted on her face. Was she smiling like a fool?

What a difference a few hours made.

She'd hardly slept last night. Yet she wasn't in the least bit tired. But needing to be alone, she was about to escape into her room and sketch those contours of Devraj's face, when Baboola's tense voice reverberated from the kitchen.

"You've learned nothing from your marriages, Eliza. When will you learn to control your urges and stop jumping from one wrong man to the next?"

"Both my husbands were Jewish, but didn't seem to be Jewish enough for you and Papa, but now I don't care." Aunt Eliza sounded almost calm. "I want to have a baby."

Almost paralysed, Lia sneaked a peak from the dim hall into the kitchen, spying her pale-faced grandmother shaking her head.

"Oh, my God, are you pregnant?" Baboola's scraping chair startled Lia.

The absent answer hung in the air. Shoulders sagging, Baboola held the edge of the table standing unsteadily. Lia wanted to run and help her sit back down.

"Oh, Eliza." Disappointment met mourning silence.

"I'm nearly thirty-six."

"Your age is no answer." Baboola almost whispered.

This was Lia's reality; the death of an unformed friendship with a wrong man, but this wasn't the time to think about herself.

Abandoning her new overnight bag and raincoat where she stood Lia rushed into the kitchen.

Both pairs of eyes stared at her. "Lia," they said.

She stared at the two dearest women in her life, feeling more ancient than them both; one wise beyond sixty-five years, and her defiant aunt, who no longer seemed as sophisticated, exuberant or confident.

"Baboola, do you need to lie down?"

Secrets shimmered in the silence. Baboola's sigh sounded like a pressure cooker in the stuffy onion and tomato infused kitchen.

She helped Baboola gently into her chair. Sitting back down with a glazed expression Baboola said softly, "Don't worry, my angel. Everything will be fine." Was she reassuring herself?

Then, looking at her daughter she added, "We won't talk about this in front of Papa. He'll have another heart-attack."

Aunt Eliza stared at her and finally nodded.

Her grandmother's heart-wrenching expression brought back the few poignant memories they'd shared with her of their hard lives and sacrifices before immigrating to England. Now their self-absorbed younger daughter was demanding understanding.

Breathing in courage, embracing her grandmother from the back, Lia said, "My lovely Baboola who's always there for everyone." Kissing her salt-and-pepper colored head, Lia inhaled her grandmother's familiar scent of basil and mint.

Baboola leaned into Lia's hug. If anything happened to either of her grandparents, she didn't know if she could survive it.

Baboola patted Lia's forearms, with small curved fingers. "Everything happens for a reason. We are healthy and live in freedom, a paradise compared to our lives in Uzbekistan, and I thank God for *you*, Leah. You're a loving and grateful granddaughter. Such a blessing, my angel."

Baboola stood up slowly, straightening her slight frame. Stiffly, she faced her daughter. "You're our daughter and we love you, but Papa and I will never attend this... this wedding, if you go through with it." Baboola visibly shook herself into her composed housewife mode. Then she turned her back to her.

Aunt Eliza reached out to her mother, who wouldn't turn round.

"Help me make dinner, Leah. The potatoes, my angel." Baboola's wavy smile betrayed an undercurrent of more impending tears in the privacy of her bedroom.

"Bye, Lia." Lia entered into her aunt's waiting arms. Aunt Eliza enveloped her against her generous bosom, holding her almost desperately.

Was Lia going to end up making her aunt's mistakes? Had she nearly started something on the same path, this weekend?

Guilt at her ingratitude at the best aunt in the world, made her bite her lower lip. Without her aunt's help, she wouldn't be attending college, or enjoying this kind of weekend.

And who fought in Aunt Eliza's corner?

No one.

Lia left the sanctuary of her aunt's embrace and rushed back to clasp Baboola's shaking hand. "Baboola, you've never met Alex, he's a nice person. What if he is the right man? You always say our happiness is the most important thing for you and Dedda."

Snatching her hand away, Baboola held it against her chest. At her stricken expression, Lia asked herself what had propelled her to speak such nonsense. She may as well have confessed she was converting to Buddhism.

"You're too young to know what you're talking about." Then with mutiny in her eyes Baboola almost growled, "You see what you're doing, Eliza? You're filling your innocent niece's head with these things. I'll never forgive you if she... No, she's not like you." Baboola turned away from her daughter, and picked up the knife with her arthritic fingers.

Tears welled up in her aunt's dramatically made-up eyes. "I appreciate it, Lia. Don't get involved." Obviously forcing a smile, Aunt Eliza picked up her handbag and flamboyant red designer coat. She looked so alone.

Why couldn't everyone get along? Torn between needing to protect her grandparents and understanding her aunt's need to live her own life, Lia still understood her aunt seeking their approval.

Watching her aunt leave, she knew this was her sign to stay away from Devraj.

Despite all the good intentions, when Lia entered the campus the next day, to watch Ella perform at the inter-university contest, Lia could only concentrate on Devraj's contribution to the show. She hadn't been aware he was involved, never mind that he could dance so amazingly. Despite the two beauties on stage with him, one bejewelled from head to her jingling ankles and adorned in a classic sari and the other in a fiery red flamenco dress, Lia could only focus solely on Devraj.

Ella's moving, pitch perfect violin solo placed second. Lia wasn't surprised that Devraj won the contest with the sexy, polished routine combining the steps and emotions of the Indian ancient kathak and classic flamboyant flamenco dance styles.

She sighed like a groupie. Was there anything he *did not* excel at?

Ella didn't seem too put out placing second. "Congratulations, Devraj. I suppose I should be pleased that you entered the contest solely to raise money and awareness for the many orphans. Is it just in India or…"

He shrugged, his breathing almost back to normal, "It's international, but there are thousands of orphans in one small part of India…" Devraj's eyes skimmed Lia's face, as if glad to see her and her impressed expression.

Listening to him, and his passionate commitment, something within her changed.

All her yesterday's intentions disintegrated. She simply wanted to be Devraj's friend, and to enjoy herself. She wouldn't think of her grandparents or even her parents' spirits right now.

Like a melting candle swaying and remoulding its rigid form towards Devraj, Lia stopped fighting herself.

Over the next few weeks, she never lied outright to Baboola and Dedda, but her omissions of what she was doing or where she was going and with whom, gnawed at her conscience.

As Christmas neared, she was grateful Devraj never mentioned anything about 'destiny' or 'signs' after that first week.

But, just because Devraj made her feel vibrant and intriguing, how could she continue playing this game of roulette? If anyone saw them, the Jewish community would have a field day. A gossip nightmare. But most importantly, her grandparents would be devastated.

Despite knowing there was no future in it, Lia still couldn't wait to spend every spare moment with Devraj.

She seemed to turn into a different person the moment she

entered the huge campus. The girl her grandparents trusted was a far cry from the wilful, young woman who only thought about how alive and beautiful Devraj made her feel.

Chapter Nine

Nearing Christmas, Lia spent even more time with Devraj.

"I wish Jimmy was half as interested in me as Devraj is in you."

"Be careful, Ella."

"Aren't I always?" Her nineteen year-old friend sounded like a woman of the world.

"Sometimes things happen..."

"I make sure it doesn't. I won't fall for a guy like Jimmy. I'm enjoying life. If anyone should be careful, it's you. Devraj's exceptionally smart and he's a determined guy. Don't get into deep water," Ella warned in her musical voice, over the noise of the busy cafeteria.

"*Now* you warn me?" Lia smiled, "Devraj and I are good friends."

"Yeah," Ella clucked. "You should see yourself light up when you're with him, and the way you go on about him...." She shook her blonde head.

Lia's shoulders and back tensed; she suddenly felt cold. "Do you think my grandparents can see the difference?"

"Sounds like they're preoccupied with your aunt, right now."

As always, tingling with anticipation to see Devraj, guilt swaddled Lia once more. She fidgeted, "I can't believe how old fashioned they are. All that matters to my grandparents is that Alex isn't Jewish."

Lia didn't like Ella's enigmatic expression. "And that's why nothing can come of your so-called friendship. Especially as they're pushing you even more to see Howard."

"I don't want to think about him." She almost shuddered. "I can't imagine him touching me, never mind..."

"When will you divulge *that* to your grandparents?"

"I don't know. I didn't say I'd marry anyone, just that I'll think about it after I finish the art degree. And what if Howard isn't as interested to settle as they say?"

"Wishful thinking, Lia," Ella smiled, "Why wouldn't he want a perfect, young bride he can mould? The problem is he doesn't know you're besotted with a sweet-talking Bollywood hunk." Ella's naughty smile shone. "But I warn you he's not your average guy you can have fun with and then move on. Devraj's intense—like you, Lia."

"Devraj understands about our different cultures, and for the hundredth time, we're just good friends." Lia's chest constricted again. "We're not doing anything wrong, and we're never alone."

When she felt Devraj's presence, excitement brewed within

her.

"Are you complaining?" He leaned in towards her, smiling that dimpled smile. "You made the rules. I'm just keeping my word." He sat beside her. "Hi, my favorite friend. And you, of course, Ella."

Ella stood up, looking around. "Where's Jimmy, anyway?"

Devraj's eyebrows rose. "Haven't you tired of each other yet?"

"Why?" Ella's eyes narrowed.

"Just... wondering." Devraj looked ready to change the subject.

"What did he say about us?" Ella paled.

"Nothing. I know you can look after yourself, but he's not as trustworthy—"

"He's beginning to see things my way. And how can you say that about your own best buddy?"

"I'm your friend, too, and I don't want to see you hurt."

They all knew Jim was a free spirit, which Ella believed herself to be, too.

"Maybe I just want to be his friend." Ella's eyebrow arched, a haughty smile on her face. "Like you two."

Lia blushed.

Devraj shrugged and said gently. "Still, you've been warned."

He was so brotherly, Lia's pulse jumped erratically. A sexy protective hero she felt all sorts of emotions for, all far from sisterly feelings.

As their friendship blossomed, over the following weeks Lia became more creative in her art projects and little white lies, or rather omissions to her grandparents about how she spent her hours after class, 'studying in the library.' She blamed her preoccupation and silence at the dinner table on the increasing amount of assignments and keeping up with the curriculum. Her studies and, so far, excellent marks showed her growing inner and outer confidence.

Apart from the one niggling thing. Their neighbour Aunt Miri's youngest son, Uri, who'd seemed to be a 'live and let live' type, lately was sending Lia disdainful looks whenever they crossed paths at college. Or was it her guilty conscience prickling?

Although Baboola mentioned Rena and her grandson, Howard, more frequently, they only came over for one Friday night dinner. On that single occasion, Lia was so nauseous from nerves she didn't need to pretend to feel sick. She'd excused herself from the table as soon as she could.

Since then she'd talked with Howard at synagogue, whenever she had no choice, and kept their conversations short, polite and non-committal.

In addition to spending every spare moment on campus with Devraj, these days she had also managed to evade going to synagogue with her grandparents on *Shabbos*, with almost weekly excuses of headaches and stomach aches. Instead, she'd sit in the hallway talking to Devraj on his car phone, miles away, until hearing her grandparents' house-key in the door.

On campus, slowly drifting away from the others, they spent increasing time together.

With Valentine's Day only two weeks away, and midterm exams looming, the campus community hall was abuzz with more activity than usual.

When agreeing to meet Devraj on Monday and Tuesday of reading week, Lia felt like a tramp. But it was heavenly being able to spend uninterrupted hours together, rushing through the rain or huddled up in a corner of the tiny Chinese restaurant they'd found weeks earlier.

Watching the rerun of the popular "Four Weddings and a Funeral" in the deserted cinema, Lia didn't mind when Devraj put his arm close to hers on her chair rest.

Until now, he'd kept his word and never touched her.

She couldn't remember much of the film, hardly breathing, melting inside at the divine feeling of being near him. From his frequent glances, she knew he felt the same.

But again, the day after Lia's midterm Art History exam, Jim joined her and Devraj in the cafeteria and tried to bring them down to earth. Looking at them quizzically, he'd raised a light eyebrow. "So, next you're going to start skipping classes and getting behind in your work?"

"Definitely not." Devraj said emphatically at the same time as Lia said, "No."

"Just don't ruin your chances." Turning to Lia he added, "Dev has to keep up the good grades; this last year's crucial."

"You're talking boll—crap." Devraj said.

"We're just good friends." Lia added. "My studies are

important to me, too."

But they stared at Jim's retreating back, each with their own thoughts. Lia jumped when she heard someone's clanging tray drop a few feet away.

"We're fine, Lia." Devraj said. She looked at his hand near hers, almost smiling at how obviously he wanted to touch her.

"We're adults who know what our studies mean to our futures."

He nodded with a vulnerable expression, which made *her* want to touch *his* hand.

Getting up she said, "I have to run, before Mr. Hutchins makes me rewrite that paper on expressionism."

Gathering her things, she caught Devraj's wistful look. "I wish I wasn't going to India. I'd rather spend that time with you."

"I have lots of studying and sketching to get on with." She'd miss him terribly, too, when he'd leave in two weeks.

When she was with him, all she cared about was the present. Even her passion for her art dimmed. Taking short walks in the abandoned, freezing park with naked trees for company, or if they huddled in the quiet corner of a coffee house, everything glowed and imprinted magical moments on her memory.

Soon that was all she'd have of Devraj, memories. Would he end it or would fate intervene? The thoughts were unbearable.

As if picking up on her dark mood, Devraj studied her. "What are you thinking?"

She smiled, shrugging, "Nothing important."

She had no one to confide in about her growing feelings for

him, not even Ella who was too self-absorbed with her music and her latest project: runaway-Jim.

Lia felt the cold chill, which had nothing to do with the damp winter, imagining Devraj and her grandparents in the same room. Proverbial hell *would* freeze over before *that* happened.

She was certain Devraj's parents didn't have a clue about her existence. Or, maybe they expected their son to gain experience of the world before settling down. Many times she was tempted to ask, "Have your family already chosen you your bride from your own culture?"

But never dared.

"Will you be all right, when I'm away?" Devraj asked.

They'd miss each other, but friends didn't voice such intimate thoughts.

"I'll be fine."

"How is it at home?"

She glanced away from his astute eyes. "Aunt Eliza seems confused about what she really wants. And when she comes over, Baboola and Dedda blackmail her, plead with her to see reason, and when she leaves, they argue with each other."

The sense of foreboding at Aunt Eliza's impending wedding was parallel to Lia's growing turmoil and ever-present guilt and fear bordering on paranoia that any moment her world would shatter or at least change forever.

Devraj frowned. Was it obvious to him, too, that this friendship, wherever it went, was doomed?

"They won't even consider Alex, because he's not Jewish."

Devraj shook his head, sympathy shining in his eyes. "In our family it's the same. This need to stick to their own culture runs back thousands of years. They want us to assimilate yet stay true to the old ways. How can we when most of us are born and brought up here?"

"If they had their way, they'd arrange a match for my aunt, too."

He sat up, eyes alert. "Too? Have they tried to set you up? I thought you said that at the beginning just to get rid of me." His possessive look made Lia bite the edge of her lower lip. The butterflies made guilty swirls in her stomach.

"No, I won't let anyone get in the way of my plans."

He became silent, almost brooding.

"How does it work in your family?" She asked, partly to sway the attention from her own family and out of deep curiosity.

Was he avoiding looking at her? "If you mean if marriages are still arranged in our family, yes, they are." Glancing at his watch, still averting his eyes he stood up. "Shall we go? You'll be late. When can we meet later?"

"I don't know. I think we'd better take what Jim said seriously."

"What the hell's wrong with everyone?" Devraj frowned. "I want—need—to see you."

After a moment's hesitation, she nodded. "All right, at three thirty at the library, but not for long."

"No, I'm sick and tired of that place. I want to talk."

"All right, we'll go for a walk."

"Coffee."

"Are you sure?"

"Friends can have coffee together, can't they?" He sneered.

"What's the matter, Devraj?"

"I'm sorry." He ground out the words and signed, raking his fingers through his hair. It fell back over his forehead. Stubborn, straight and beautiful, like Devraj. She sighed.

"It's this damned trip. I don't know how you can be so calm about not seeing each other for such a long time."

"But it'll be such an adventure. I wish I could go to India."

He looked as if he was in pain. "I wish you were coming with me, too." Then the naughty grin took over his features. "I could smuggle you in my luggage."

"And be rolled out of an ancient rug straight at your father's feet, like Cleopatra at Caesar's feet." But her smile disappeared at the vision. Was the head of an empire tall and awe-inspiring? Devraj's father was probably respected and adored by his family and the community.

Would their paths ever cross? She shivered. And was Devraj tense because his family were arranging his marriage, too?

The heavy weight on her heart had nothing to do with the weight of her books. It was a good thing they both knew their friendship could go nowhere. Nobody would ever understand or accept it.

Watching the worry cloud Lia's expressive eyes, Devraj felt like a hypocrite. For weeks, he'd racked his brain to find a way out of going to India, knowing what his family had in store for him.

Did his parents suspect he was interested in a secret girl? Like Lia's, Devraj's own world was a tightly knit circle with plenty of eyes and exaggerated gossip.

But his parent's would never force him to marry. He wasn't ready, yet he visualised possibilities with him and Lia creating a life together.

Well, once he figured out a clearer, practical path to their joined future.

He could see in her eyes her unvoiced questions, but he didn't know the answers. The precarious situation haunted him, and he couldn't even contemplate the viability of Lia's family setting her up with some Jewish guy.

Dev had to find a way to bring Lia properly into his life and future. Maybe on their trip, his father would be more approachable. Somehow, Dev doubted it. Maybe he could find a way to stay.

Chapter Ten

THE NEXT DAY, Devraj's mood was considerably lighter, once more being the fun guy Lia knew and loved, in the 'friend' kind of way.

He didn't mention the impending trip and she didn't ask whether he'd return an engaged man.

They were having lunch at the local burger place with Ella and Jim. Pushing slightly away from Ella, Jim teased Devraj, who'd recently been approached by a modelling agent.

But Devraj gave his friend the 'drop it' stare.

Ella glanced from Jim to Lia. "Aren't you proud of your b— friend, Lia?" She cooed at Devraj's sexy scowl.

Lia was still amazed at how unaffected Devraj was by his looks and dancing talents. The males around them usually tightened their hold on their girlfriends, whose eyes followed Devraj as they passed.

Now Ella's poutiness and the rising tension between her and Jim distracted Lia again. Almost ignoring each other, the once-affectionate Jim now acted like a caged animal.

In the bustling restaurant, Lia heard Ella say to Jim, "I need to see you alone, Jimmy, just for a few minutes."

"No, give it a break, Ella, and I'm Jim, not Jimmy." The clang of his cutlery brought attention from the couple sitting at the nearby table.

Lia sighed. They were arguing, yet again.

"Trust me, it's important, it's the least you can do for me. I need—"

"You need, you need—" Jim bit out. "What are you, my wife? I owe you nothing." Jim threw his napkin on his half-empty plate and stood up. "I've had it. It's over."

Ella's lower lip quivered, tears glazing her large eyes.

With a deep sigh, Jim apologized to Lia and Devraj and strode away.

Devraj touched Ella's hand. She looked up as if in a daze.

The sympathy in his eyes must have been too much, because she shot up and, with an agonized whimper, fled the restaurant.

Lia stood to follow her, saying to Devraj, "I'll see you at four at the same place."

Lia was half an hour late but Devraj looked relieved. "I thought you wouldn't show."

"Ella needed me. I hope she'll be all right."

"Let me drive you home, Lia."

"No way." She shook her head vehemently.

Studying her, he nodded. "All right, I'll walk you to the bus stop."

"N-not a good idea."

"Please, I want to." If they were seen together, they risked far too much. But in a few days, end of February would tear them and keep them apart for six whole weeks. Anyway, these days Uri, the neighbourhood gossip's son, didn't even look her way.

She sighed shakily, "All right."

As they left the building, huge rain clouds swirled above them like dark gray ruffles of a flamenco dancer's skirt. Rumbling thunder sounded too close for comfort. Lia hated thunder, but felt strangely safe with Devraj.

"Let's make a dash for it." He said over the wind, his arm around her waist. It felt so natural and delicious, like in her constant dreams, that she didn't move.

Inhaling sharply, Devraj let go as if she was a hot poker. "Is this it? Are you going to slap me and send me away?"

His vulnerability made her smile. "No." She shook her head and rummaged in her bag. "I have an umbrella. You should go back to your car."

No sooner did she have the little umbrella out than huge cold drops started falling on them.

Dev caught Lia's sketchpad as she opened the little gismo. Laughing, he felt free, like everything was right with the world. "You call this an umbrella? It's a handkerchief. Agrrr." He ducked as the rain glued his hair to his forehead and temples, and felt his shirt soaking through his open coat. "That went down my collar and it's freezing. True friend you are, keeping yourself dry and letting me get soaked." He shuddered dramatically until she looked up at him with those gorgeous eyes.

"I can't help it if you're a giant." She giggled making him want to laugh aloud.

Hearing her laugh he knew how much he'd miss it. His gut wrenched every time he thought about having to leave her for so long.

"A giant! I'll have you know—"

She trembled beside him. "Stop it, now's not the time to defend your ego, I'm getting drenched, too." Thank God, she seemed to have lost her earlier tense demeanor. He'd feared Jim and Ella's breakup would make Lia rethink their friendship.

They ran the rest of the way to the small bus stop, and scooched into each other under the crowded cover it offered. When she leaned closer into him to protect him from the rain, he felt himself grow hard.

If he touched her, like in his dreams, he'd never let her go.

"Well, I'm a true friend and I insist you stay under your umbrella. I'm a man, I can take a little freezing rain. Come here for a moment." Leaving the huddled people at the stop, he pulled her into the relative darkness of the doorway of the poster-covered, abandoned storefront. Looking behind her, her smile disappeared, as if she hadn't been aware of the shallow enclosure. God, he wanted her so badly.

Suddenly Lia felt closed away from the world. She stood glued to her corner and Devraj, obviously taking advantage of their predicament, imprisoned her in the too-intimate circle of his large arms. Even in the graying light, his eyes glinted with mischief as he looked down into hers.

"You're such an opportunist." Her breathy voice shuddered.

"What did you say?" He almost whispered, leaning into her as if inhaling the scent of her hair. The familiar fresh smell of Devraj's damp skin and cologne made her almost dizzy. She nearly closed her eyes, but didn't dare.

"You can't accuse me of ordering the downpour and inventing this doorway just so we can be this close." His warmth, his voice, his tentative stroke on her forearms through her clinging coat played havoc with her senses.

She gulped at his growing intensity.

"You don't have to be this close. And don't h-hold me." Could he hear her heart pounding in her chest?

"Do you really want me to let you go?" His lips skimmed the side of her wet head, her temple, sending warm tingles through her body.

She was about to lie when the thunder blared. Gasping, she pushed a palm against his chest feeling his warm skin and rigid muscles under his shirt and unbuttoned coat.

He felt so inviting; she closed her eyes.

Who was the opportunist now?

Maybe this was a dream, literally a wet dream.

"Stay with me for a moment longer, Lia." His confident smile was almost predatory. Surrounded by this storm, no one else existed with their prejudiced ignorance and fears.

"You look like an angel, a sweet angel." he said, "Will you

always look at me like that, all our lives together? Say it, Lia, tell me you feel it, too—because I—"

"No, Devraj. Don't." Her urgent voice shook again. She yearned, yet feared, to hear his next words.

"Why not? I'm in love with you, Lia, and before you make a run for it—" He grabbed her arms, staring down at her like a king. "Admit it, neither of us wants to fight this powerful force between us."

For as long as she lived, she'd never forget those words and that look. She closed her eyes to stop staring at him. "You're crazy." She sounded weak, feeling as hot as melting wax.

"Yes, Lia, I am." His voice was gravelly, a sound of torture she understood too well. Daring to open her eyes, she realized her mistake.

Who was she kidding? How long had she been fighting these chilli hot, fiery emotions? And, from his look, Devraj felt the same.

Chapter Eleven

"I'VE BEEN DYING to say it; I love you so much it burns my insides. I can't bear the thought of being away from you even for one day. Kiss me goodbye." Devraj stared at Lia's mouth, making her lick her dry lips.

"Why? A-are you never coming back?" Her insides quaked. If he weren't holding her, she'd have been a wobbly mess by his feet.

"Don't even joke about that."

"You—you aren't leaving for another week."

"Then you'd kiss me if I was leaving tomorrow?"

"No, Devraj." Her voice sounded frantic in her ears.

Imperceptibly, he leaned into her, his mouth gravitating towards hers. Suddenly she wished she were taller, desperate to feel those lips on hers immediately.

Then, he was kissing her.

Mesmerized by the need in his eyes and his demanding lips, her eyes fluttered shut again. She moaned, moving into him.

How she'd dreamed of this.

No more lying to herself. Melding into him, her body knew what she needed better than her mind did.

Her bag forgotten by her feet, her hands rose up his broad chest, reveling at the muscles flexing under her touch. Her arms wrapped around his neck. Their lips spoke their own natural language. Even the roughness of his cheek and jaw added to her pleasure.

Lia loved him.

As the thought ping-ponged through her whirling mind and thudding heart, his tongue licked the inner corner of her lower lip, setting her on fire.

When his tongue sought entry, her eyes shot open.

She froze.

He pulled his mouth away from hers, seemingly breathless, too. Without loosening his grasp, he looked at her. "I've wanted to kiss you for so long, Lia. You're really in my arms." He pressed his body against hers.

His voice, his bulk, his virility frightened her. But even more, her own reaction, her intense need for him, overwhelmed her. Breathless, she pulled back, with nowhere to go.

Everything reeled around her. Had the world turned upside down? With the wall behind her, she attempted to push him away.

He wouldn't ease his hold. "I've never felt like this. You smell so good, like peaches and... hmm." He leaned into her. She felt his powerful thighs against hers. He smiled softly, his lips so near hers, as if about to take another drink of nectar, rightfully his.

"No." She evaded his mouth, praying the rain would let up, and yet fearing it would stop too soon.

"How have you become so important to me in such a short time?" His voice was seductive. "Admit it, Lia, you want me, too." He pulled her closer. Loosening her already-mussed waves from the ponytail, his fingers sent magical shivers through her scalp down her body.

She was about to nod and even let him repeat that wonderful, toe-curling kiss, but his words penetrated her trance.

He wasn't supposed to say those things. They couldn't love each other.

An image of her grandparents seeing her in this man's arms, dropped her down to earth, and cold reality.

Once again, she heard the wind and traffic swooshing by, feeling a slight, cooling spray on her face. The torrential rain, like a dam of diamonds all around, hammered against the concrete pavement a few inches away from their feet.

Fear fuelled her strength, pushing Devraj away with hands that had held him for dear life only moments ago.

"Let me go. Now."

"It's only a matter of time before we—"

"No. You've spoiled everything." Scorching tears coursed down her already-damp face.

He looked as if she'd struck him. "What?"

"Because of this..."

"There's no pretending and I'm glad, because I love—"

"No!" She almost shrieked against the thunder, echoing too loudly in their cocoon. "Now there's no going back to being friends. A true friend wouldn't put me in this situation."

"Don't deny this. I see your love in your eyes. Feel it in your kiss, your touch. You can't live without me, either. We'll make this work, Lia. I'll talk to my father and if... the worst comes to the worst, we'll elope."

"You *have* gone crazy." She shrank away, finally loosening his grip. "You sound like you're in a bad Bollywood movie." She shoved him away from herself. "Let me go and don't come near me again."

Grabbing her bag, she ran out from the enclosure, getting even more soaked without her umbrella.

"We'll see who won't be able to stay away from whom." His confident words followed her through the biting wind and rain.

With an excruciating erection, Devraj tried to compose his equilibrium. Why did it feel so perfect when he was with Lia? His lips curved as he rushed back to his car. The onslaught of the rain did little to serve as his proverbial cold shower.

Patience, he reminded himself. He'd give her some time to collect herself. Maybe a day or two, no more. He couldn't bear losing precious days away from her, with the trip looming over him. *If* he ended up going to India.

They needed time to take control of the growing intensity of their attraction. But just as he'd known how sweet and tantalizing her kisses would be, he knew nothing would be the same between them.

Still shivering after the hot bath Lia had escaped into two hours earlier, she was huddled in her bed, knees drawn up under her chin. It was dark, but she didn't want lights on, yet.

She was no better than the easy girls she and her grandparents condemned. How could she have enjoyed such a sensual kiss? She blushed remembering it, yet, there had been a sense of inevitability in their every word and touch.

She couldn't blame Devraj; she was livid with *herself.* But, now she'd pushed her luck on so many levels, including risking being seen with Devraj. Her days of playing with fire in the guise of the Bollywood-gorgeous devil were over.

Sad but necessary.

She prayed she wasn't too late with her revelation.

Her grandparents had enough worries without her adding to their burdens.

<h1 style="text-align:center">Chapter Twelve</h1>

WHEN LIA RETURNED to college two days later, having gotten over a cold, Devraj seemed to be everywhere she went.

But he never looked her way. When she spied him having lunch with a girl from his original group, and heard him laugh, she told herself she'd had a narrow escape. He was obviously making up for the wasted five months he'd pursued a scared-y-cat.

Good riddance, she kept saying to herself, desperate to regain some semblance of interest in her studies and her appetite.

After reliving the kiss through another restless night, now her anger overshadowed all other emotions. His persuasive tactics had made her fall for him so darned easily and naively, she had believed all his passionate, whispered words. Boy, he really was a good actor, after all.

Now replacing her with another girl, a blonde, almost as tall as he was, Devraj was no better than the fickle Jim.

Tempted to go to Devraj and slap him—hard—in front of all his friends and groupies, she reminded her ego that he was free to play wherever, whenever and with whomever he pleased.

Lia would clear her muddled brain and heart of all thoughts and naive feelings as if *he'd* never existed.

Now her life would be peaceful again. No more lies or furtive glances over her shoulder. She'd burn all those romantic drawings along with her stupidity and gullibility that could have jeopardised everything.

Oh, God, she'd left her sketchpad behind when she'd escaped Devraj in the rain.

When her eyes searched Devraj's whereabouts, she caught him watching her before smoothly turning his attention away. She'd rather die than ask him for the pad. Most of the work was of him anyway. She held on to her indignation like a cloak against other less welcome emotions; like disappointment and missing the charmer she'd become so attached to.

Well, she'd get over it.

Anyway, soon he'd probably be married off to a perfect Indian bride. She quelled the heaviness the thought brought to her heart.

As Lia absently opened her fresh sketchpad, she jumped like an escaped criminal at the sound of the familiar deep voice.

"How long are you going to play this game?" Devraj came into her peripheral vision.

"Don't creep up—" She whispered, resisting the urge to put her hand against her galloping heart.

"Have you come to your senses, yet?"

"Yes, thanks. I realized this week how lucky I am I didn't end up like those other girls. Once you get what you want: complete surrender. That's all you guys are after. Now I'm back on track and *not* in the market for a 'friend.'"

Devraj's silence and narrowed glare weren't a good sign. She knew him now, unlike when they'd played at being friends. One rain-soaked kiss had opened her eyes, and shot her dreams to sensual overdrive; damn him!

"Don't compare me to others and stop talking as if you still don't know a damn thing about me. You're just running scared. And I saw that guy sniffing around you again this morning. It's worked. I'm jealous. All right?"

"What?" Realizing whom he meant, she added, "Adrian and I are just friends." Guilt prickled. Why couldn't Howard or any other man make her feel half as intriguing as Devraj had? Would she ever feel this alive, this crazy again?

"So you're getting on with your life while I—" He raked impatient fingers through his hair. He glanced up at the ceiling and then scanned her face again.

She guarded her heart from softening at the tired lines on his face. He was nothing to her. He was her first kiss, that's all.

"I meant every word I said." He said in a low tone, taking a tiger-like step closer, leaning into her. It took all her resolve not to budge from her seat. "So you'll hear me out."

He grasped her forearm. She pulled away and got up. Her chair grazed the floor loudly, but she didn't care. "Don't ever touch me." Collecting her things, she marched towards the lifts, confused at Devraj's lack of action.

Then striding beside her he gripped her arm and pulled her past the lifts towards the emergency exit doors.

"I'm warning you." She glanced over her shoulder for any familiar faces.

No one cared. Fear and exhilaration warred within her.

"And I'm warning *you*, Lia." With unnecessary force, he pushed open the emergency door with a broad shoulder, leading her to the narrow window, which flooded the stairway with winter sunlight.

Letting her go he stared. "Get off your high horse and bring down that chin."

She stared back, trying in vain to calm her erratic pulse.

"Grow up, Lia." Too close to her again, his arms imprisoned her on either side.

How she'd missed him, his scent, those hungry topaz eyes on her. Soon he'd be in India and this sexual attraction between them would dissipate and bring them back to relative calm.

She prayed.

"Listen carefully, Lia." His chest rose and fell, a tiny nerve at his jaw pulsed. "I love you and I want to be with you. I've waited for you to admit it, too. I don't give a shit about the differences in our backgrounds or family cultures. But *you* grab the first chance to push me away, again. It was one kiss. And you wanted me as much as I wanted you. Instead of spending every moment together, you've been hiding like a scared mouse, while I haven't been able to sleep or eat." He let her go, as if to stop his words. "Just tell me what I can do to prove I'm not playing games."

She could hardly breathe. "You know i-it'll never work."

"No, I don't and you don't either. What will it take to break down those archaic barriers?" He caressed her arms, as if unable to hold back from touching her, studying her as if trying to remember her every feature.

"Nothing." She tried to push him away, but in vain.

"I can't imagine life without you." He pulled her into him. He was near tears. This intensity was no act. "I refused to go to India, I want to be with you."

Her body weakening, Lia felt faint. She shook her head, bemused.

"Last night my parents told me they want me to meet this girl, a business partner's daughter, in India."

Jealousy pulsed through her veins like venom. She swallowed, but he wouldn't let her look away.

"But I refused. I told them I'm in love with someone else, and I'm serious about her. I warned them that if they pushed me, I'd leave home. In case it's not clear, I love *you*. Marry me, Lia. You're not a coward; inside, you know you're mine and I know you also want us to spend the rest of our lives together. Starting right now."

Her tears distorted his intense features. She only managed a sob. He'd spoken to his parents about her.

He was staying; he was proposing.

As if knowing her legs were giving way, his arms clamped around her even tighter, and she felt home.

His spicy cologne, intermingled with the unique musk of his

skin, were emblazoned on her psyche. His heart pounded an ancient drumbeat of need, his muscles sizzling against her hands. "Tell me you love me, too, Lia. I can't bear life without you... without this heat between us." He kissed her as if the world was about to shatter around them.

A languid yearning washed over her; its cavernous ache throbbed within, leaving her filled and yet hollow.

As he kissed her again, her limbs turned liquid and she leaned against him, moaning again. "Oh, God, Devraj, I..."

"Yes, Lia? I'm yours."

Blinking away tears so she could see him, she touched his face and welcomed his sure hands from her waist up her spine, to her shoulders.

Gently he cupped her face. His fingers intertwined in her hair, loosening it, until its heat against her back further raised her temperature. He kissed her cheeks, temples, wet eyelids.

"I'm sorry I doubted you, Devraj. I don't want to fight it anymore. I love you... too." She breathed out, closing her eyes as the incredible words echoed around them. No more denial. How alone she'd been, as if in limbo until she was with him again.

Their joint relief was liberating.

He kissed her as if he was drinking in life itself. Now she saw hope in his eyes. He laughed softly in the echoing quiet. "At last, my Lia. Nothing else matters but this—how we feel about each other."

She was thirsty for that feeling of completeness yet every touch and kiss left her hungry for more.

The world stood still.

"You'll see we belong together. Our families, Jewish, Hindu, none of that matters. You'll always be mine. I feel like such a sap, but I don't care." Tears glistened in his eyes and he smiled. "Promise never to let anyone come between us."

She nodded, absolutely certain of their love. He made her insides clench in that strange way, as if she was one of those heroines within the pages of her own gripping love story. But this was so much more powerful. This was real.

The image of her grandparents shot through her mind. The shivers and the heat crawling up and down her spine had nothing to do with the cold metal and glass of the window against which she was resting.

Again, she pushed away everything but this moment. Warnings and fears disintegrated as she stared at Devraj. This vital prince with flashing white teeth and deep soulful eyes was the only thing that mattered.

Life without him no longer existed.

She blinked away tears. "I promise, Devraj. No one else matters."

She welcomed his deep kiss until the knot in the pit of her stomach melted and her insides throbbed. Moaning, she was desperate to touch him, to let his tongue explore and teach her how to kiss him back, deeply, without reservation.

Tightening her arms around his neck Lia watched him shyly, and marvelled at the warmth in his eyes. With shaking fingers, she explored the planes of his shoulders, his warm muscled neck, his Adam 's apple, and jaw. Everywhere she touched, her lips followed.

Something between them changed.

She felt as if she'd loved and kissed Devraj all her life.

He was her one and only love. Her one and only destiny.

Chapter Thirteen

THE FEBRUARY SUN shining on Devraj's face set aflame the hunger in his eyes, sending waves of hypnotic pleasure through Lia.

His touch became bolder. Whispering, "My Lia, I love you," as if he couldn't have enough of hearing and uttering the words. His hands played their own magic on her overly sensitive skin. His lips trailed warm kisses from her swollen lips down her throat, to the gentle hollow above her breasts.

Instinctively, she raised her head to meet Devraj's mouth, to relieve the gnawing urgency between them.

Lowering his hands to her waist and hips, his breathing became ragged. His touch faltered for a moment. "You've driven me crazy, Lia. I want you so much." His eyes asked her if she'd run again. "You'd better stop me *now*, because *I* can't. I'll—explode into a million pieces."

Afraid he'd stop, she kissed him fervently.

Drawing her closer against his hard body a sound akin to

relief and a chuckle whispered against her mouth. He sucked on her swollen lower lip while pulling away her warm coat off her shoulders, letting it rest behind her. Then he grasped her bottom and gently lifted her a couple of inches onto the window ledge on her coat. His hands lowered to her back, exploring her curves through her thin cotton blouse and wool jumper, and down her long jean skirt.

Her breasts felt heavier, the craving nipples erect against the hard wall of his chest as her back pressed into the cold window.

Holding her gaze captive, he allowed a sliver of space between their torsos. Wedging a sinuous thigh between hers, he slowly separated her shaking legs. Goose bumps trailed through her melting body.

Gently, he stroked her long hair, lowering until his fingers hovered by the front of her blouse.

Like an angel poised to strum a harp.

The dull ache within her sharpened as his lips warmed her skin, sending heated shivers of anticipation through her.

Pleasure erupted as he tenderly rubbed his thumb against one covered, craving nipple. Desire descending into the pit of her abdomen made her hungry to play out the natural dance of their love. Their lips, tongues and fingers explored, their moans echoed in the abandoned stair hall.

Lia welcomed the cool air greeting her heated skin as Devraj slowly undid each button of her blouse. Closing her eyes, she leaned back.

Half opening her eyes, his hunger and appreciation made her

momentarily stop breathing.

"You're so beautiful. Your skin's like hot silk." He growled softly against her throat.

Reverently he pulled away one cup of her bra out of his way. She sighed feeling his breath against her breast. And at last, he took a nipple in his mouth. Her unsteady fingers explored the contours of his flexing shoulders through his shirt.

"Let yourself feel; don't analyze, Lia." His massaging thumbs roved sensuously from her hips to her midriff. Her insides coiled. His touch grew more intimate, demanding her to kiss him back.

"I need you," he ground out hoarsely, "now and always." Gently pulling up her skirt his sure fingers burned a trail up her thighs. When he found her most sensitive and secret spot, her moist centre craved him. Her breath caught as he pressed his manhood against her thigh, as if gravitating to her heat.

Nothing else mattered but feeling this loved, this alive.

He fumbled with his jeans for a moment, his features rigid with passion. Then, slowly she felt his heat against the most intimate part of her as he stared with heavy lidded eyes that kept her captive. "Don't worry, Lia, I'm protecting you, all right?"

She nodded and swallowed through her dry throat. Combing her fingers through his crisp hair, she brought his mouth down to hers again.

Releasing her lips a fraction he almost whispered, "It'll hurt only for a minute, Lia. Trust me, I'll make it good for you."

His touch distracted her too much. The way he separated

her legs wider. Then within seconds where his hands had been, he was slowly filling her up with his hardness, all the while touching her softness and kissing her, until she understood what it would feel like to almost spontaneously combust. The pleasure was so new yet so natural. They were even breathing in unison.

Then a searing pain tore at her insides. She cried out into Devraj's mouth, her eyes wide as burning pain shot through her.

He stopped, concern in his face. But as he continued kissing her, within seconds his soft, encouraging words and his touch brought the ripples of sweet hunger back.

Then within moments pleasure transported her into a new world of such torturous joy she started to breathe deeper.

Her eyes fluttered shut, holding him hard. Her body welcomed Devraj's slow and deliberate thrusts, wanting him to get even closer to her, into her.

Lia knew she could never be with anyone else. With tears in her eyes, she vowed to make this love last all her life. Their hearts seemed to race in harmony, together.

She gasped, suddenly rising up a mile-high mountain on wings of ecstasy, too frightening yet freeing. Gripped by convulsive waves of bliss she moaned, breathless. Then she felt Devraj's body tense and heard his feral groan which made her feel at one with him.

"I'll always love you, my Lia, my precious angel." His chest rose and fell against hers as he panted and smiled. Kissing her, he held her so closely she heard his heart beat frantically against hers.

His sweat-sheened arms surrounded her protectively as he whispered against her ear, "I'm sorry. Are you in pain?"

Slowly opening her eyes, she shook her head, although she was.

She looked at the semi clad Devraj. Had she pushed away his jacket to the ground behind him, had she undone his shirt buttons, to feel his hair-roughened golden torso?

"I didn't mean to rush you. I couldn't help myself, but I really wanted our first time to be so special." He sighed and smiled sadly, "You deserve the perfect romantic first time in between silky sheets and low lights. I'll make it up to you, my Lia. The next time—"

The perspiration on her body cooled at his words.

Fear punched Dev in the gut as patent shock and something else registered on her face. He tried to hold her closer to him, but she gingerly lowered herself onto her feet and pulled her blouse together. She *was* in pain. He hated seeing unshed tears shining in her eyes. "I'm so sorry, Lia. I couldn't help myself."

She shook her head, still refusing to look at him.

"It was meant to be, right?"

She nodded as her lovely swollen lips trembled. She seemed unsteady on her legs. So was he, come to think of it.

Giving her some space to let her compose herself, he straightened his own clothes, tucked in his shirt and put on his jacket. He knew she loved him, but had this been too much too soon for her? Not *only* had he taken her virginity but also trust didn't come easily to her.

"Lia, you will marry me, won't you?" Damn, wasn't it the girls who usually sounded so clingy? He didn't care if he sounded like a romantic idiot. What else mattered if he lost her?

Having donned her coat, she breathed deeply, her mouth trembling. "I want to, but what if we can't? It's not just us..."

"We're destined for each other; we love each other, that's all that matters."

She said nothing, just closed her eyes. He pulled her against himself, loving the unique scent of her. "Let's meet at Ella's place tomorrow. We can make plans and I want us to be together. I'll show you how special—"

She cringed away from him, "I don't feel right about—"

"We can go to a hotel, I just didn't think you'd want that."

"I have to go home, Devraj."

"It's important, please try to get away for a couple of hours. I'll see you at twelve at the same place on the campus. You said you love me; hold on to that, Lia. It'll all work out, I promise you."

His repeated words seemed to calm her. As if letting out a long-held breath, she nodded and slowly gave him a wobbly smile. She looked at him the way she had when she'd admitted she loved him too. "I'll see you tomorrow." Despite her shyness, he loved seeing a new confident glint in her eyes, as if she finally trusted him.

"You *can* trust me. I'll take care of everything."

Dev loved her, Lia loved him. That was all that mattered.

Chapter Fourteen

AT LAST, LIA stopped fighting her all-consuming attraction to
Devraj. He was the only man she'd ever want to be touched by,
the only one she'd ever love.

Hugging the huge secret to her heart, last night Lia had
found it difficult to stop smiling at the dinner table, or raising
her eyes to either of her preoccupied grandparents. She'd
excused herself to her room as soon as she'd left the small
kitchen sparkling clean.

Still unsure how she was going to face Devraj in a few
minutes, she blushed at the flashbacks of yesterday's special
moments they'd shared. It still felt ethereal.

Her world was changed forever. Now she really belonged to
Devraj, body and soul, God help her. What a hypocrite. How
could she think of God who'd created her as a Jew, while she
was irrevocably in love with a non-Jew?

She pushed away the familiar sense of doom in case it
escalated into a heart-palpitating panic attack.

She was about to meet Devraj and although it was a lovely sunny day, the cold wind pulled her away from where he usually waited. They were going to Ella's place, to be alone. She'd never missed a whole afternoon of classes, but all she wanted was to be alone with him. Suddenly she felt thirsty.

She heard her name called out. Slowly she swiveled to face a tall, grey haired, distinguished man. The haughty nose and full lips seemed familiar. His eyes, darker than Devraj's, took her breath away.

He stared down at her. "Are you Lia Abraham?" His lilty accent reverberated in patriarchal tones she recognized from Bollywood movies. She nodded, tempted to step back from the man's regal aura.

She swallowed, looking around, praying she'd see Devraj, yet fearing she wasn't supposed to be associated with him.

"I'm Amit Shah, Devraj's father. Can we talk for a moment?" He pointed to the imposing dark car a few feet behind him. Only now, she noticed the uniformed chauffeur standing beside it, his hand on the car door handle.

Instead of shaking her head and running, she willed her legs towards the now open car door.

"I assure you, you're quite safe." The tight, condescending smile wasn't reassuring.

As he sat opposite her in the opulent interior, the smell of expensive leather and Mr. Shah's impeccable appearance highlighted how different their worlds were.

This was Devraj's life, his legacy.

"I'm sure you're a busy young lady." Had he hesitated on the word 'lady'? "So I'll come to the point. Last night Devraj told me about your ... relationship, but I wanted to meet you and ask about how *your* family feel about ... all this."

Even Devraj's name was more possessive on his lips. Its authentic sound belonged to the empire built and raised by the Shahs.

Her heart thumped against her ribs, her hand jumping to her throat. Suddenly she knew their relationship had no chance.

Never had.

After all, could she imagine this man in the same room as her grandparents. Never, and she'd rather die than cause them grief by telling them about her love for the idyllist, romantic Devraj.

"Your silence tells me you haven't broached the subject with your parents." He was very patient, she thought numbly. He could afford to be. She was no match for him.

"My family's view on tradition is the same as yours—"

"What do *you* know about tradition?" His sudden anger awoke Lia out of her apathy, making her cringe. Anything was better than the withering hope ebbing out of her.

"My sons are our legacy. They *will* carry on the family business and *will* marry the girls chosen by us, their elders. There's no room for you in Dev's life."

To her, Devraj was the fun-loving, passionate, intelligent guy. But he was a prince with too much ancient responsibility. Whether he liked it or not.

"And if he's got carried away by his libido, then I warn you to protect your honour and don't let this get out of proportion. You'll suffer unnecessarily." He paused, as if weighing something. "Has Dev told you he's engaged to a girl from back home?"

She couldn't catch her breath. Her inner tension revving to overdrive threatened to choke her. She couldn't hold back her betraying tears as much as she hated them.

The elder man shook his head. "*That* is his destiny. You're smart; you must have known there's no future in this."

Why couldn't you have come yesterday? She wanted to scream and scratch at him. Anything to stop drowning in helplessness.

The silence stretched while Lia's vision blurred and all her silly hopes in her heart burned to cinders.

But instead of opening the car door to announce the end of their conversation, to let her lick her broken spirit, Mr. Shah leaned forward.

She gasped as if facing the grim reaper.

He pulled back. "Having met you I can see why Dev is so captivated. But it'll break too many hearts, if you don't stop this immediately. He's impulsive, a dreamer, my Dev. You're both still quite young, and if you do something rash, in time you'll resent each other. *You'll* ruin his whole future. And your family, would you not miss them? Would they ever forgive you?"

She pursed her lips.

The pain shadowing his eyes left no doubt about his stance on this. "It would kill Dev's mother, with her heart condition."

A sigh as heavy as her grandparents' worries emanated from him. Then he straightened his bulk.

Having refused to look her grandparents in the eyes, now she was facing the enemy who possessed calm and ultimate power. Claws of claustrophobia grew oppressive.

Lowering her head, she closed her eyes, as more tears leached out, and wished she could die right here, right now.

"Help Dev see reason; you must end this, now. His future— our family's future happiness is in your hands. Goodbye, Lia."

Hearing the door open and getting the gust of wind, which whirled inside the car, she blindly let herself out.

Within seconds, the car disappeared as silently out of her life as it had entered it. One short meeting with a stranger turned her world on its axes again.

For what seemed like hours, she stood immobile in the cold more tears streaming down her face. The sun went on shining, life continued while her heart splintered by the jagged wisdom of Devraj's father's words.

Acute shame and fury at life's unfairness shattered into one another.

It was already too late; she was soiled goods. Having given in to her strong sexual urges, she'd begun believing in the strength of their love. This could cost her family their respect in the community if anyone found out.

It could kill Dedda and even Baboola.

Burdened by Devraj's father to do the right—the only— thing, Lia had to throw out all her foolish convictions of twenty-four hours ago.

God give me strength. Her watch showed she was twenty minutes late. She shuffled her way through the small uncaring crowds towards the bus stop, in the opposite direction of where Devraj was probably still waiting.

She couldn't face anyone, especially him.

She'd lost her head, her heart, and virginity to the idealist. It would hurt like hell—even deeper than her physical soreness and emotional agony—but she'd do what she had to, and be strong for them both.

Yet the prospect of surviving without the love of her life was like cutting out her heart and still trying to go on living.

Chapter Fifteen

FEELING INCREASINGLY SICK, Lia brushed away errant tears and with only steps away, she squinted at crowded bus stop with no bus in sight. Her heartbeat went into overdrive when Devraj's red sports car stopped beside her.

He opened his window, looking at her. "What happened, Lia? I waited... Please get in."

"I need to get home." She pulled her coat tighter.

Devraj's hopeful smile crumbled. Ignoring the hooting cars behind him, he parked and dashed out towards her, his brows furrowed. "You're so pale, what's wrong?"

There was nowhere to hide. "Please go before we're seen together." An older woman next to her watched them.

Lia didn't care. But she knew she should have.

"But I thought you could skip—"

"No, Devraj. I won't skip anything."

"What's happened?" He studied her closely. "Is it your grandparents?"

She shook her head and avoided his gaze. She could never tell him about her visitor.

"Look at me, Lia." His voice rose and she looked around, conscious of further curious glances following them. "I want to be with you." The hunger in his eyes brought warmth to her cheeks.

"No." She looked away.

"I said look at me." Taking her hand, he pulled her towards the abandoned alcove where they'd kissed days earlier.

He grabbed her shoulders. She welcomed the distracting discomfort from the cold roughness of the wall against her back. She wouldn't look into his eyes; she'd see his father there.

"What's the matter. If it's about yesterday..."

Closing her eyes, she gritted her teeth and her fists clung to her hips.

He manoeuvred her chin so she'd meet his eyes. Even in the shadows, his face held too much emotion. Pulling away from him, a sound of a trapped animal escaped her. More tears came.

He let her go suddenly. She nearly fell. Instantly he was supporting her again.

"Please don't cry. Talk to me, Lia. I'm sorry, I should have thought... We'll take it slow, we can just talk, make plans—"

When she kept shaking her head, "No! I *have* to go home."

Dev studied Lia. His heart thumped against his ribcage so fast he was sure she could hear it. "OK, let's talk somewhere quiet for a minute."

Lia flinched from his touch and he backed away, fear

gripping his insides. He swallowed the disappointment that they couldn't be alone, to make love in a proper bed, as she deserved. How often he dreamed of having her under him, passionate and completely his, as she had been yesterday. Uncomfortable heat prickled his insides.

"I spoke to my father last night. I couldn't get out of going on the trip, he wants me to meet business contacts, but they won't be setting me up with anyone now. They know I'm serious about you. Please don't look so hopeless." He wiped away her warm tears, feeling her quivering.

"Don't give up on me, on us, Lia. Wait for me, we'll get married when I come back..."

She didn't respond, merely stared at him as if all his words were lies. It killed him that she still doubted their love. How could she have reverted to her fears after yesterday? It was obviously connected with her grandparents.

Shutting her eyes tight she recoiled again when he reached out to her. He needed her close, he'd miss her badly, but Lia didn't seem herself. Her ashen face told him she wasn't well. The tremble of the mouth he ached to kiss, added to the haunted look in her eyes, before she closed them again.

Stop being selfish and protect her. How could he reassure her she wasn't alone? Obviously, the gravity of yesterday's lovemaking had been too much for her, after all. They'd have plenty of time to be together after he returned.

"Meet over the weekend, if you're too tired right now. I'll explain everything, my parents just need more time to adjust to this relationship. For now I'm just grateful they've been surprisingly tolerant to the news."

Lia realized Devraj was oblivious to his father's strategies and manipulations. At least her grandparents were honest about their plans for her. Nevertheless, she could not blame Mr. Shah for getting Lia do his dirty work; he didn't need to destroy his bond with his beloved son—while Lia was expendable, dispensable.

That truth hurt.

Despite her head throbbing, and unable to see properly, she forced herself to kill all ties with Devraj, right this minute.

Her heart racing, she stared at him. "Stay away from me."

Her fury seemed to throw him off.

"Don't come near me again. I told you from the beginning this isn't going to work, but you kept pushing. Now you got what you wanted, so stop hounding me." She prayed her expression was cold and firm. She bit the softness of her inner lip, raised an eyebrow for good measure, and added, "We both got what we wanted."

Shaking his head, he glared at her as if an alien possessed her.

"You're saying *you* used *me*." His voice was flat, his eyes narrowing.

"Yes." She glanced towards the bus stop and the waiting people.

"Look at me. Why are you lying?" Desperation grew on his face.

Unflinchingly, she looked up at him, the pain from her finger nails digging into her palms kept her from changing her mind. "Can't your ego handle the truth?" She paused deliberately. "Sure, I was curious about sex, and maybe I just wanted to get rid of my v-virginity. Thought about that? But now I'm going back to my real world. My art, my own family, my own plans."

He let her go again. She leaned back against the wall.

"I don't believe a fucking word you're saying. Stop this and tell me what's happened. Tell me what your grandparents did, or are you just a coward?" He searched her face.

She clamped her lips and again shook her head. The volcanic volatility in his eyes made her want to throw her arms around him and kiss away the torture she'd inflicted. But hardening her heart, she looked steadily into his eyes.

"You don't know what you're doing right now. You'll miss me before I'm even on that plane. You'll come begging to me, but then it may be too late for us."

"Good. Then you'll finally leave me alone."

He closed the space between them, imprisoning her with his body, his eyes hypnotizing her as if he knew he could conjure up those same emotions he had yesterday.

But with Mr. Shah's last words ringing in her ears, she didn't respond to Devraj's contact.

When the heat and weight of his body left her, she felt desolate. Opening her eyes, she saw him turn away, his head low.

But, like a man shackled to her by invisible chains, he didn't move.

The shocking hiss of the breaks of the bus was never more

welcome to Lia. As she pushed past Devraj, she heard him say in a voice that left no doubt he hated his own weakness, "I'll wait for you at Ella's tomorrow."

"No." She got on the bus and grabbed its pole like a lifeline.

"Then Saturday... or Sunday. Try to get away. I need to see you before I leave. Please, Lia."

But she could never look back.

Chapter Sixteen

UNCARING ABOUT FELLOW passengers, Lia hung her head and cried. Reality had come down on her like a ton of rubble, and she had lied to Devraj. How could she have believed they had a chance, ever? Just as he had no idea of his family's power, she'd underrated her grandparents' wisdom. They loved their daughter and granddaughter dearly. They'd gained much wisdom in their long lives. She cried harder.

Lia needed to talk to someone, but she couldn't voice her shameful secret, even to Ella, who was hurting, too, right now. After the initial state of denial, Ella was devastated about Jim's rejection. She was even neglecting her studies, and had backed out from next week's long-awaited violin contest.

Lia quelled her urge to confide in Aunt Eliza. What could she say? *I gave my virginity to the only man I'll ever love, but I can't spend my life with him because no one will accept our different cultures.*

In this suddenly grey and murky world, she knew that was

the only certainty.

She'd been selfish enough already. Now, she'd suffer alone.

"Who was that boy Aunt Miri's son saw you with earlier?" Baboola confronted Lia as she opened the front door. Groggy and numb, her heart still went into overdrive. So, the gossip had already reached her grandmother even before Lia had arrived home. Uri, the snitch. He must have driven by and witnessed, or even heard the commotion.

What had she expected?

"You've been crying? What's happened?"

Lia turned away from Baboola not to witness the panic in her eyes.

Not now, please. Ask me in a month, a year. It may feel less raw by then.

"Nothing, Baboola." Lia said with no conviction or interest. What was the point? She could never face Devraj again.

A sob burst from within her chest up her burning throat.

Aunt Eliza rushed in from the front room. "What happened, my angel?" She threw an accusatory glance over her shoulder at her mother while hugging Lia.

Lia would never forget the suspicion and disappointment in Baboola's eyes. "You've been acting very secretive these past weeks, now tell me what's going on."

"Nothing's going on, Baboola. I promise." She said flatly.

"You're promising now. Shame on you. Aunt Miri says Uri told her about seeing you and this... boy in that college many times. Have you been missing classes and spending time alone with this... boy?"

After a split second's hesitation Lia replied, "I spent some time with him, but I'm not anymore." Now she understood how Aunt Eliza felt whenever Baboola stared at her like this.

"I need to lie down. May I please go to my room?"

Baboola sighed, making Lia hate herself even more. She'd lost her distressed grandmother's trust and brought pain into her eyes.

She closed her eyes, head bowed.

Still reliving the older Shah's words and seeing Devraj's betrayed expression, Lia wanted to bury herself away and never see or speak to anyone.

"Dedda and I have suffered so much to give you the best life we can and here you are bringing shame to our family and yourself." Tears glinted in her old eyes before she turned away.

Lia gaped, helpless.

"If she said there's nothing going on, then trust her." Aunt Eliza said. "You've always trusted her."

"We also trusted you again and again. You see! I told you she'd be influenced by you, watching you—"

Aunt Eliza gasped. Lia wrenched herself out of her aunt's protective arms, stepping toward her grandmother. "Please don't blame Aunt Eliza. I promise you I'm never seeing... him, again." Then drained, she hurried up the stairs on cumbersome legs.

Aunt Eliza would come up soon and let Lia bare her soul. But right now, she had a love to mourn. Alone.

The open romance book on her bed mocked her. Picking it

up she hurled it across the room. Pages packed with lies and promises, hit the wall, and scattered on the carpet.

Who was the writer kidding? Women reading this drivel were in for a rude awakening. As Lia knew now, there was no happy ever after for her love for Devraj in this lifetime.

She'd never forget him and would always be grateful to him for making her see herself differently. Beautiful, graceful and unique. They'd borrowed from others' futures, and now she'd face her life with eyes wide open and her heart bandaged tight.

How she'd get through the next few months avoiding Devraj on his return from India, she didn't know. More tears overwhelmed her. She didn't care if she could be heard.

Staying in bed into the evening, she refused to go down for Friday night dinner.

Aunt Eliza came up with a full plate. The food's familiar smell and the thought of eating it made Lia's gnawing stomach revolt. As soon as her aunt put the plate down on the desk, Lia threw herself into her waiting arms.

Her need for comfort outweighed her shame or hunger. Slowly, between hiccups and groans, she told her aunt everything, omitting only the single time she and Devraj had made love. Lia needed to obliterate the memory as much as she yearned to encapsulate it.

"I'm sorry to be such a cry-baby, Aunt Eliza, I know you've got a lot on your mind, but I don't know how I can survive without Devraj, and yet just imagining leaving Baboola and Dedda..." A deep sob vibrated from her heavy chest and grazing her raw throat. "Oh, God, tell me the pain will stop."

Her aunt listened to her, stroking her clammy head while rocking her like a baby. "Unfortunately I can't promise it'll stop hurting," Aunt Eliza whispered into Lia's hair. "But I know with time the pain *will* lessen, although right now it's hard to believe."

In three long days, an airplane would take Devraj to his destiny, far away from her. She'd learn to survive one day at a time, like an addict who knew the stakes.

Once more, she wished she were dead.

Eventually she fell into a sombre sleep, still enveloped in her aunt's arms.

The following morning waking up alone with a drumming headache, still far from hungry, she couldn't muster any strength to leave her bed. She left the curtains drawn, intermittently crying, and falling asleep. She imagined Devraj waiting, even felt he was sending strong signals her way.

When she refused to eat or talk to Baboola or Dedda by three that afternoon, they called Aunt Eliza to come back.

Whispering soothing words of hope, reminding Lia she was young and strong, Aunt Eliza cajoled her to come down to the kitchen and have a bowl of Baboola's chicken soup.

Washing her hot, blotchy face with cold water Lia breathed in deeply, but her lungs wouldn't cooperate.

Why bother breathing? Even art seemed like a distant, childish whim. All she yearned for was the one thing, one love she could never have.

She felt her grandparents' worry from across the table. Once again, she bit back her drowning emotions. Having managed to have half of her soup, she breathed in deeply.

It still hurt, but no more tears.

Declining her aunt's offer to take her out, Lia absorbed herself in reorganizing and sorting out her room. She tore to shreds the pile of mementos and notes from Devraj, but her hands wouldn't obey when she grabbed the numerous sketches of him. She tied them up in the black art binder and shoved them behind the bags of the untouched clothes in which she'd felt like a frump, when seeing herself from Devraj's eyes.

By seven that evening her hands were red from scrubbing and cleaning the bathroom until everything sparkled. But she preferred to feel this kind of exhaustion than the bone-weary sense of doom she'd wallowed in for over twenty-four hours.

Lia was about to ascend the stairs to hide in the dark room, when she heard Dedda talking to her. She turned back to see her grandparents in the hallway.

"Howard's coming at eight, to take you out for coffee."

Lia stood statue-still, the walls of her prison closing in.

"Are you listening to Dedda, Leah?" Baboola asked.

"I'm sorry, I'm tired, and I'm not interested in meeting anyone."

Her grandparents exchanged concerned looks.

Calmly, Baboola said, "We know how important your art is to you, Leah, but Howard's also ambitious and he told his grandmother he likes your independence."

Lia's numb senses on alert, revulsion and apprehension prickled her all over.

"Mrs. Kooland knows the Goldman family and now that he's settled into his new practice, he wants to get married and have a family." Baboola sounded as proud as if he was her own grandson.

"I'm not ready." She looked at Baboola, who wouldn't look at her properly.

"We know you're ready for marriage, Leah." Dedda's firm tone defied argument. "To the right man."

"If this is because of... the other guy, I promise I'll never see him, a-and he'll be away, abroad—"

"Good." Baboola said and Lia realized it was no use talking. She couldn't blame their determination to marry her off. She now appeared to have joined the delinquents she'd heard them discussing at the dinner table since she was little.

She couldn't be trusted anymore. She was lucky they hadn't forbidden her to go back to school. Or would it not look right to Howard and his family?

Dedda fidgeted with the pages of his worn, leather-bound *Tehilim* book in his hands, his bushy eyebrows casting a shadow over his aging eyes. "Do you know how lucky you are to make this kind of match?"

"Yes," Lia said, "but I want to finish college and then look into a job in a private art school in Par—"

"You can do all that after you're married." Baboola said.

"It's all settled." Dedda donned his ancient reading glasses and turned away from Lia.

Aunt Eliza quietly cleared her throat. Lia had almost forgotten her aunt was still here, silently observing them.

Baboola folded her fleshy arms over her sagging bosom. "This does not concern you, Eliza. Don't complicate matters."

Aunt Eliza said, "I was going to say that maybe Lia will have a nice time." Ignoring her mother's surprise, Aunt Eliza softly said to Lia, "It'll take your mind off other things."

Lia sighed, knowing her wise aunt—despite not being so wise on her own personal issues—had a good point.

It was eight on the dot when the doorbell rang. For a crazy moment, she prayed it was Devraj, then could have kicked herself.

Lia came down the stairs slowly. She'd showered and left her nearly dry hair down. At Baboola's gentle request, she wore the new royal blue cashmere top that seemed too bright against her sallow complexion in the mirror. She'd paired it with a long, black skirt and low pumps, as Howard wasn't that tall.

Her heart beat frantically as if Howard would instantly see she was no longer the pure girl she'd been a few days ago.

Chin up, she opened the door to the man who had no idea she felt forced to go on a date with him.

Chapter Seventeen

THERE WAS NOTHING unattractive about Howard. He was charming and opened the car door for her, holding the huge golf umbrella over her in the pouring rain. But he couldn't help that he wasn't Devraj. Lia shook herself inwardly, listening as he talked about his work and family. He was a couple of inches taller than she was. His sandy coloured hair, slightly thinning on the top, was immaculately combed. His blue eyes were not as warm as Ella's. He was entertaining and engaging, but again Lia wished she was alone in a dark room with her memories.

"So, you're studying art." Howard stirred his milky coffee in the quiet corner of the café he'd chosen.

She nodded, aware she wasn't as forthcoming with her end of the conversation. But talking about her passion seemed a betrayal. She breathed in and slowly exhaled, "I'm doing a three year arts degree. Then I plan to teach." Why wasn't she mentioning the rest of her plans about travelling across Europe, starting with Paris? Did she know deep inside it was another pipe dream?

"That's great. I bet you're good with children." He didn't wait for an answer before adding, "I come from a traditional background. My older brother runs his own computer business and he's been unlucky in love, but now he's married again, with a child on the way. My mother holds the family together." He smiled again, the perfect son describing the ideal family. Lia had only met his grandmother and father, who seemed very nice and quiet. But did the mother not care about attending synagogue? "I'd like you to meet them. My father likes you already. You're like a perfect, exotic doll."

Mistaking her discomfort—she didn't think she was exotic—he leaned over his coffee, his thin lips twitching.

She couldn't imagine those lips anywhere near her. "I'm sorry, I thought you're used to being told how beautiful you are. It's endearing, your shyness."

For a moment, she feared she'd burst out crying or worse, blurt out that she'd never be interested in him.

Imagining her grandparents being embarrassed in front of the Goldmans helped her pull herself together. She looked down at her untouched coffee cup. "Thanks. I'm sorry, I wasn't ready to meet anyone, but my grandparents..." What would he say if she asked, *would you still be interested in me if you knew I wasn't a virgin?*

But the coward that she was, she stayed silent.

"I know, my grandmother was hounding me, too. And my parents want more grandchildren." He smiled sheepishly. "But the more I saw you the more I wanted to get to know you. I know I'm a few years older than you, but I've got excellent prospects and I'll look after you in every way possible." His sincerity was admirable, but left her cold.

"But you don't know anything about me, Howard."

"So, here we are, getting to know each other." Then, his eyes lighting up, he told her more about his new clinic.

The next day, Sunday, near midday when the phone rang, Lia froze in mid-motion, with a scrubbing brush in her hands over the toilet bowl. Filled with guilt for not warming to Howard, and feeling cheap and unfaithful to a lover she'd never see again, tightened her breathing airways and her breaking heart.

What if Devraj had the crazy idea of phoning her to demand she meet him?

It was Ella. She sounded her usual self, but Lia may as well have been facing her friend, reading her thoughts. "So I need to see you for a short time, Lia, erm, can you come over?" There was a pause where the mouthpiece was obviously covered. "Or do you want me to pick you up?"

She was so tempted it was disgusting.

Closing her eyes, she concentrated on sounding casual and firm. "I'm sorry, Ella. I'm still not feeling well. I'll see you tomorrow."

"Lia, it's me." She gasped at Devraj's voice. "Please, Lia, don't put the phone down. Listen, I have something very important to tell you. I have to see you. I'm missing you already, I'm going ape-shit, waiting. Please come outside your house in twenty minutes. Ella can give me your address—"

"No." Her shrill voice made Dedda look up from the other side of the room, Baboola raising her shrewd eyes from the sewing project on her lap. "I'm sorry, Ella, I can't go anywhere today. Have a nice... break."

"Why are you punishing me for a trip I can't—"

"Goodbye."

"Lia, don't you dare—" Devraj's voice blared as she put the phone down. For a frightening moment she was certain he was going to drive here and bash down the door.

She prayed Ella would be sensible and not give him her address.

Sitting in front of the TV next to her grandparents, she could hardly breathe. Until late that night, she imagined the scenario where all hell would break loose if Devraj turned up. She jumped at every phone call, passing car, certain this was the straw that would break her grandparents' patience, and they'd lock her up in her room forever. For her own good.

What if Devraj did *not* go to India tomorrow? She wished and feared at the same time. Her life was complicated enough without her conflicting thoughts and betraying emotions.

Only the next afternoon did she breathe a tight sigh of relief. For the next six, long weeks, she'd do everything in her power to stop obsessing about Devraj. She prayed that by the time he returned she'd have grown a backbone to become immune to him. All she had to do was replay her conversation with his father in her mind.

Ella seemed even more subdued and distracted at college. Resentment grew at how easily Jim had crushed Ella's spirit.

He strutted around like a peacock with girls as his ammunition.

Unable to pry or come up with something helpful to say, Lia knew when her friend was ready to open up to her, she'd be there to listen. Ella had always done the dumping, never looking back.

In the meantime Lia's period was a few days late.

Fear gripped her. It had always been regular. She had to stop imagining crazy things. Stress would do that. She reminded herself of how much had happened within the past two weeks. Not only had she had her long fantasized first kiss, she had also experienced her first...

She stomped at her veering thoughts.

Only after she promised her grandparents again that 'the unsuitable boy' was actually away for a few months, they loosened their vigil over her every move. However, she suspected that Uri was still put in charge of keeping an eye on her.

She was sure that her acquiescence at meeting Howard went some way to appease and reassure them she was back on the straight and narrow.

Aunt Eliza, on the other hand was getting the brunt of their disapproval as March brought a beautiful spring full of daffodils and tulips.

Her aunt's civil wedding ceremony was to take place next Friday and the arguments continued.

Poor Aunt Eliza.

Chapter Eighteen

THE NEXT DAY Aunt Eliza ended up in hospital. She suffered a miscarriage. When two days before their wedding, Alex left without warning, her aunt was devastated. At her stoic grandmother's insistence, she'd moved in with them, and the whole house seemed shrouded with such despair Lia thought she'd never regain her faith in God again.

Accepting Ella's invitation to visit her on Saturday at the end of March, Lia looked forward to catching up with her best friend properly. For the past weeks, she'd missed the old fun Ella.

She needn't have worried about Ella grilling her about Devraj, because her friend seemed lost in a world of her own. As they made their favorite homemade macaroni and cheese, Ella dropped the carton of milk on the kitchen floor and burst out crying.

"Don't worry, accidents happen, Ella, I'll help you clean up."

Shaking her head, Ella hid her face in her hands and

snivelled. "Accident! Oh, Lia, I'm so afraid. I'm pregnant."

Lia gasped, had she misheard? But it all made sense. "Oh, Ella. Does Jim know? Is that why…?"

"No, and before I could, he dumped me in front of everyone." She ran to the living room and threw herself on the couch, her sobs vibrating through the pillows. Lia wanted to find and kick Jim in his cowardly, immature guts.

"I'm so sorry, Ella. If I'd known, I could have been here for you. What will you do?"

"I don't know." Ella sighed, blew her now pink nose in another tissue Lia had given her.

God, what if *she* had been faced with this dilemma? Lia shuddered at her immense relief and at the same time wondering 'what if'… when she'd got her period nine days late.

She held her friend and listened.

"I can't think straight. Yet I want the b-baby, and worst of all, I still love Jim." Ella cried harder against Lia's shoulder, her body wracked with her sobs.

"Everything will work out, you'll see, Ella. I'll help you."

Howard had been coming over the past few Saturday evenings. Lia was civil and polite, but her mind kept veering away. The only things Howard and Devraj had in common were their sense of confidence and going after what they wanted. Their families seemed very close, too. But where Devraj planned to pursue his passion for architecture, the older Howard was already doing exactly what he'd set out to do; his calling clear and his ambition awe-inspiring.

On April Fool's Day, when he brought her back from their dinner date, outside her door, when he reached for her hand as if to kiss it, she cringed away.

The confusion marring his features left instantly, making her ashamed for being so rude.

"I'm sorry, Howard, I just can't seem to feel as strongly..." She couldn't help feeling nothing for him.

"It's all right. I may be traditional, but I'm not old-fashioned. No pressure. I'll wait for you as long as you want. Well," he grinned, "I'm not getting any younger." He had a high sort of laugh.

Lia forced herself to smile. "Thank you," she turned towards the house, hoping she didn't seem overly eager to leave him.

Again, she stopped the question that burned in her mind. Why hadn't Devraj returned yet? But hadn't she refused to pick up any calls from strange looking numbers?

Maybe he'd been married off like in those Bollywood movies.

So what? Hadn't she needed time to strengthen her resolve for the inevitable end? Surely, with the distance and family influence, Devraj also realized by now it had all been futile; that he'd just got carried away with their sexual attraction.

Chapter Nineteen

TWO WEEKS LATER, on a warm but wet May Monday, when Lia was convinced Devraj had immigrated to India permanently, she caught her breath as she entered the cafeteria. Devraj stood with his back to her, speaking with the smiling Ella and the subdued Jim who had his arm around her waist.

As if instantly aware of her presence, Devraj turned to Lia. He seemed changed somehow, more reserved, manlier and more handsome with a deeper golden hue to his skin. His eyes seemed brighter but guarded.

His lips curved in a cool smile as she approached.

She should have been glad of his aloofness. Their two lives were like oil and vinegar, never to blend even with a good shaking. Though they lived in the same world, even side by side, they would be forever separated.

Obviously, Devraj was accepting that. Now she could move forward, too.

Watching the rose blush on Lia's face, Dev knew she was underplaying her excitement at seeing him again. He had missed her so much, he ached.

But before she'd reached him, she turned to leave, and his intentions to stay away until *she* came to *him* disappeared. "Wait."

She stopped and stared at him through thick lashes.

He wished he could pull her into himself in front of everyone. He appreciated Ella and Jim giving them a wide berth.

"I'm sorry I shouldn't have called that Sunday, but I waited all weekend. You didn't even call."

Her eyes told him she'd hoped he wouldn't bring that up. Her lower lip quivered as she replied, "I couldn't. A lot's happened since you left."

His heart drummed again. "Such as?"

"My grandparents found out about us that day by the bus stop, and I was more or less under house arrest." She hesitated.

"I'm sorry; I didn't know, Lia."

"Then Aunt Eliza had a miscarriage a few days later and her fiancé abandoned her two days before the wedding."

"That must have been hard on you all. I'm sorry." He stopped himself from nearing her.

"Of course it's also been tough for Ella, until they made up. I know she still loves him, but I'm not sure if Jim's ready for m-marriage."

Avoiding her question, he said, "Jim told me what a little mother tigress you were, telling him a few home truths. He didn't even know Ella was pregnant."

Dev almost smiled at the memory of Jim recounting Lia's stormy expression, when she'd said, "For someone who's supposed to be so smart, *Guinness*, you sure are dumb. Why don't you grow up and take responsibility for your actions. Help her make the right decision, either way, but just do it together."

Dev wouldn't tell Lia that he too had lost his temper, calling Jim "a selfish bastard" a couple of weeks ago, when he'd phoned from the small kiosk in the heat of the village his family had stayed in for an eternity. "Get your act together, Fred," Dev had said clearly through gritted teeth, "Stop hiding behind the skirts of those shallow girls. If you feel you can make it work, then do right by Ella; it was an accident and it takes two to tango!"

Now he said to Lia, "I'm glad they sorted it out and I'm sure they'll get through this together. But remember, they're very different from us."

Then changing the subject he listened to her explain about her studies, and how important it was for her not to get distracted, and instead of worrying about his own upcoming exams, Devraj stared deeper into her eyes.

But she evaded his probing eyes.

"Let's go and talk somewhere, Lia."

"We've talked now. I cannot risk being seen with you, even like this. I just wanted to say... goodbye, Devraj." She turned away.

"We can talk now, being watched like goldfish in a bowl or you meet me later. Or I can come to your house. I had your address, but I didn't come that Sunday to give you time to think, while I was away."

"I *have* thought." Agony replaced the fear in her eyes. "Please let it go. I thought we'd—"

He closed the space between them, standing a breath away, tempted to touch her. "I can't, Lia. Let's go to the Chinese place, where we won't be recognized by anyone."

"I'm sorry, I can't."

"Even for old times' sake?" He tried to smile but felt it tense on his lips.

A hesitant frown marred her delicate brow, then she nodded.

"But after that, we're—"

"Save it for later. See you at four."

She rushed away.

He couldn't concentrate on anything but being with Lia. Throughout the family trip, he'd fought off his parents' wishes to meet business partners' daughters. Respecting their honour, he was an exemplary son on all other occasions, including business meetings, knowing his family saw him as a major future asset. But he didn't care about anything but getting back home, to Lia.

They loved him and would soon realize his heart beat only for her, and that all else was futile.

Yet, he was losing her. Something wasn't right, but he knew she loved him. He'd hold on to that. It had been her grandparents as he'd suspected, but he'd find a way forward.

Time seemed to move backwards until he met the edgy Lia

at their allocated place and time at four o'clock. He was surprised she'd let him drive her to the restaurant, as if impatient to get on with it. He drove the few minutes in silence, enjoying having her so close.

As they finally settled opposite each other in the intimate booth, in the almost-deserted restaurant, he felt her nervousness escalate.

Lia kept her menu closed. "I can only stay a few minutes," her fingers tugged at her thin jacket around her chest. "This is the last time we see each other. You don't know what I've gone through these past few weeks. My grandparents forced me to—" She stopped talking, looking away from him.

Why was she so afraid? They had such a hold on her.

"If it was half as bad as what my parents made me go through, I have some idea," he said softly, "but they know I meant what I said two months ago, they know I love only you."

"Stop, Devraj. I'm not going through that again. For the remaining weeks before you leave college, *please* stay away from me."

His radar kicked in strong. Something else was going on with Lia. "While I've been going through hell without you, you're still saying the same crap?"

The waiter came, Dev quickly ordered some dishes, and when they were alone, continued, "My family said to give it time. Coming from my father, that's a *miracle*. And you're still talking about breaking up. I'm so sorry for what your aunt's gone through, but please don't judge me—or the world—on that. Tell me what's happened. Are your grandparents putting more pressure on you?"

She paled, shifting in her seat. Finally meeting his eyes she said, "It's them as well as your family. Despite what he said, I know your father will never accept this because he—" Her voice shook. She bit her lower plump lip, nearly distracting him.

"So now you know my father better than I do. Stop stalling and tell me what's really behind all this."

Taking in a deep breath, she slowly let it go, "I'm not lying to my grandparents or looking over my shoulder, anymore. I'll finish my degree and start my own life. There's no room for anyone else in it—for you or the man my grandparents set me up with—"

"What? You went out with another man?" Dev saw green. He gripped his water glass not caring if he shattered it. He ground his teeth so hard a headache bloomed at the base of his skull up his crown and temples.

"I had no choice." She averted her eyes again.

"Of course you did," Dev almost growled, trying to stop his voice from rising. "You could have sent him to hell and told your interfering grandparents you love *me*." He wanted to kill the bastard who'd taken Lia out with her grandparents' blessings.

Agony stabbed through his heart. Shaking his head, he stared at her. "How could you see another man while all these weeks all I could think of was us?" He was going to vomit.

Were those held-back tears and pity in her eyes? "You can hate me, but it was wrong from the start. We both got carried away. But I'll always be grateful that you were my first."

He smacked the glass down, grasping the edge of the table. "If I'd not been taught to respect women, I'd—" How could he still love her this much, yearning to grab her and kiss her. "I *know* all this is an act." He drew satisfaction seeing her flinch, her eyes darting away again. "I know you better than you know yourself, Lia." With swift movements, he sat beside her, imprisoning her in the booth. Grasping her arms, he pulled her against his chest.

Her familiar scent of peaches and spring-like freshness made him want to cradle her tense body into himself, forget all her words and the world and make her trust in their love again. "If we were alone right now you know you'd feel differently. Us between silk sheets, naked and hot, my skin against yours." With every slow word, his mouth gravitated towards hers.

"Stop it." Her strangled voice grated. Her dilating pupils and soft beckoning lips drove him over the edge of reason.

He kissed her urgently but felt Lia hold back.

"Open yourself up to me, Lia," he whispered against her lips before kissing her again. His tongue darted inside her warmth, and as he knew she would, she melted against him. She closed her eyes with a moan.

The kiss went on and on.

Dev felt home. She loved him, he just knew it. Holding her tight, he smiled in relief, whispering in her ear, "My Lia, despite your words, your kisses can't lie. I know you love me. Your grandparents pushed you to see this guy, I get that. I'm sorry; I just got so jealous. But you promised never to let anything or anyone come between us. Marry me."

"No." She pushed away from him, her eyes wide. "I can't. I won't deny the sexual attraction between us, and you're a great lover. You were my first, but you won't be my last."

$$Chapter\ Twenty$$

THERE, LIA THOUGHT, closing her eyes for a moment. She'd gone for the jugular.

She swallowed the growing lump in her throat at the vivid pain in Devraj's stunned eyes.

Good, she needed to sicken him, after succumbing to that kiss, needing him to hold her one last time.

"Does this guy make you feel this hot when he touches you?" he bit out. His thumbs rose gently to her breasts, and her nipples hardened under his touch, making her shudder and squirm away from him.

"Stop."

"Has he kissed you and touched you the way I have?"

She gasped, shoving away his intimate fingers. The thought of Howard touching her revolted her. "Stop acting like an animal."

He let her go and she pulled back against the wall, drained and disgusted by her own weakness.

"Are you compatible, apart from you both being *Jewish*, of course?"

Itching to scratch at his face, she shook her head, eyes closed. She had to do something to get out of here, but couldn't think straight. Then she stared at him, "Stop bullying me, this was a mistake. Let me go or I'll scream."

Again, his arms imprisoned her. "I don't care. You're not hearing me."

Pushing her fists against his chest, she felt as impotent as an ant.

"Go on, make my day, try and sock me one," he focused on her mouth as if he'd punish her by kissing her again.

"I know I hurt you. I'll always remember you, but now I have other plans." She held his gaze.

Devraj's grip hardened on her forearms and he hissed through gritted teeth, "You're a filthy, lying b—" He let her go again. He swallowed hard, as if about to be sick. "I can't believe I still want you so much, but I-I need you. Please come with me."

"Don't." Her heartbeat frantic like a caged animal's, she wanted to cry from her craving to feel close to Devraj, naked, next to her, on top of her, inside her, like she dreamed over and over. "It's impossible."

"It's not. We're in charge of our lives. We love each other."

"No. I. Don't. Love. You." She said it with as much conviction as she could, seeing his father's eyes in Devraj's face. "Stop sounding like a romantic idealist, Devraj."

"And you stop lying. Let's elope and get our own place. I'll get a position in my other uncle's manufacturing company and we can travel and do all the things we've talked about."

"No. Put all this energy into your plans for architecture."

"I don't care about anything but us. Please don't ruin both our lives. Surely, you wouldn't marry for your grandparents' sake." He sounded incredulous.

No, but I would for your sake, Lia felt like screaming. That was when the horrible realization struck her: that he'd never accept this was over. Devraj would never let her go. And if she told him about his father's visit, it would only destroy another relationship with the same end result.

They were not meant to be. No matter how much she craved it, she couldn't beg him to take her far away from this nightmare.

Because they weren't living in a fairy tale.

She went for the kill once again, "Obviously you haven't thought this through. I want a big white wedding, under a canopy with my Rabbi and my family there. That's never going to happen between *us.* I came to make sure, once and for all, you leave me alone and don't jeopardize my chances and my future."

He gasped, jerking away from her. A nerve pulsed at his clenched jaw, his lips thin.

Pale under his tan, he got up, fists balled by his sides. "I know you, Lia, and I *still* don't believe any of this crap. Stop acting and stop letting your grandparents dictate your future—*our* future. And tell this guy it's all off, or *I* will."

Fishing some note bills out of his wallet he leaned towards

her, "Otherwise you're making our love cheap and meaningless." He threw the money on the table in front of her. "Call me when you come to your senses." Devraj flung on the table a small card as if it was an ace. "This has also got my home number—unlike the coward that you are, I want you to call my home, because I know that my family *will* accept you, us, if we both just wait and bide our time. Why won't you trust me for once, damn it!" When she said nothing, he spun away from her about to march off, and nearly collided with the waiter holding their meals.

Lia heard a door shut and took in a breath. The sight and smells of the food the waiter laid in front of her attacked her gag reflex. Before she could put her hand over her mouth she vomited over the card, the plates, and the money.

Chapter Twenty One

WHEN HOWARD CALLED early that evening to ask Lia to take her for coffee, she was about to decline. But he was persistent. After meeting with Devraj earlier, she was emotionally drained. She had planned to escape into a much-needed bubble bath, and then lose consciousness in sleep. Instead, she decided to see Howard to tell him it was all a mistake.

It had nothing to do with Devraj's empty, hotheaded threats and everything to do with not leading Howard on. In its own way, it had served her purpose with Devraj, meeting Howard for the dinners and coffee dates. Now Devraj hated her, but at the same time, now she was on dangerous ground with her grandparents looking at her, as if expecting an announcement from her or Howard any day.

Marry Howard? Never! Not even for her grandparents.

But when Howard took her to their usual coffee place, she wasn't in the mood for the excitement dancing in his eyes.

"My parents have invited you for Friday night dinner." He

smiled as if honouring her with a royal summons.

"Howard, I'm sorry—"

"I think I know what you're going to say and let me reassure you there's nothing to worry about. Our little age gap won't make a difference in the long run. You're very mature, and you can keep *me* young." His thin lips twitched in a smile.

She couldn't accept an eight-year difference as 'little'. But that wasn't the point. "Howard, I don't feel comfortable seeing you and giving you the impression I'm interested in..."

"Marriage?" Howard helped, smiling again, "Am I that obvious? I was going to surprise you with a large diamond ring on Friday. I already asked your grandfather for your hand in marriage."

She felt colour drain her face. Two proposals in one day: One she'd have loved to accept, but couldn't, while the other she could never consider.

Now she knew she'd never marry anyone.

"What I'm saying is that I'm not ready at all to get married."

"OK, let's get married next year, have a long engagement." He took her hands in his. They were so much smaller than Devraj's, with fleshy, smooth-skinned fingers. She focused on his words. "Or we can get married this summer and go on honeymoon wherever you wish. Then you can go back to college to do your... degree, if you wish." He sounded like a paternal caregiver, a patient, benevolent saint.

"I have to decline, Howard. Sorry."

"I won't take that seriously. I'll let you have a few days to think about it." He said in a relaxed manner. "I'll pick you up

Friday evening."

She stood up, unable to breathe or speak.

Why would neither man take her words seriously? Instead of going into another intense—or any —conversation, she asked to be taken home.

As Howard drove off, after escorting her to the door, she sighed deeply.

Did all men suffer from selective deafness?

Wondering how to get though to Howard, the knight in a white coat who left her cold, she stood in the corridor, hearing her grandparents and Aunt Eliza talking in the kitchen. Although it was still only nine-fifteen, she started up stairs. She needed to soak her weary numb body in a bath more than ever. She was halfway up the stairs when the doorbell rang urgently, repeatedly.

Lia's instincts told her this wasn't good. It was either the neighborhood gossip, Aunt Miri, or...no.

Devraj wouldn't do anything this drastic, she prayed, paralysed with her heart pounding painfully within her ribcage.

Chapter Twenty Two

TAKING A FEW ginger steps back down, Lia gripped the stair rail, as Aunt Eliza stopped by the kitchen doorway, and Baboola shuffled towards the door.

Lia stopped breathing when she saw Devraj filling the threshold. Had her thoughts conjured him up?

Before Dedda could beat him to it, Devraj marched towards Lia, his haunted eyes riveted to her face. Standing on unsteady legs two rungs above the foot of the stairs, she watched Devraj as if in slow motion reaching out to touch her.

At her grandmother's gasp and Dedda's loud "Oy!", Lia cringed away.

"Are you seriously considering marrying that guy, when you love *me*, Lia?" He pointed into the darkness through the open door behind him.

She glared at the incredibly stupid and selfish Devraj.

"So he's the one Miri mentioned." Baboola said in Russian.

Dedda quick small steps brought him to Lia's side, also

staring up at the intruder.

From Devraj's mutinous expression and stance, Lia was terrified he'd shove her grandfather aside.

"So it *is* much more serious." Dedda's hoarse voice made her stare at him. His familiar wheezing grew as his shoulders rose and fell and his frail hand grabbed his compact chest close to his betraying heart.

Lia and Baboola gasped.

Instantly supporting her grandfather's small bulk, she shoved Devraj out of her peripheral vision and slowly led Dedda back to his armchair. Baboola shadowed them.

Helping him to sit down, Lia kneeled by Dedda's feet. "Sit down, Dedda." His sallow face grew paler. "We're getting your medicine." Her eyes followed her aunt's swift movements, who rushing to the sink, filled a glass of water, and soon held it out with a tiny pill to her father. "Here. Should we get an ambulance?" Aunt Eliza asked as if this was a normal occurrence.

Dedda shook his head.

"You sure?" Lia asked holding the glass for him while he drank.

Baboola loosened his collar, her shaking fingers fussing with the small pillow under his head, against the tall armchair back.

Finally, he nodded, taking slow shallow breaths.

"You'll be fine in a moment, Papa. Relax."

Lia inhaled deeply, letting out a trembling breath.

Something alien burst within her. She rose and faced Devraj, who stood immobile studying her grandfather with narrowed, uncertain eyes. Was he suspicious of the man whose fragile heart could again give way at any moment?

"How dare you barge in here like this? It's over; I couldn't have made it any clearer."

"Are you engaged to him?" The pulse in Devraj's unshaven jaw betrayed his inner turmoil. She hardened her heart. He nearly killed her grandfather.

"Tell him to leave *now.*" Dedda said shakily, continuing in Russian. When no one moved, he inhaled and slowly said in slow, broken English, "You do not belong here. Go back to your family, your own kind."

"I need to speak to Lia." Devraj kept his eyes on her.

"How could you do this?" Lia asked.

"Leah, how could you get involved with this...?" Baboola was shaking. "If Howard hears about this—"

"Is that his name, Howard?" Devraj demanded. "*Have* you been engaged all along?" He stood a breath away from her.

Again, before Lia could respond, her small Baboola stood to her full height of five feet and stared up at Devraj. She said with her strong accent, "Yes, Leah *is* going to marry Howard. You must leave her alone."

In her slow Russian, to get through to Dedda more than to keep Devraj from understanding, Lia bit out, "I don't want to marry H-Howard—"

"You'll do as we say." Dedda said. "Your parents would be ashamed of you ..." He stopped, reaching a shaky hand for the glass of water again.

Still in Russian, Lia said, "I don't love H-Howard. And this isn't about *him*," she inclined her chin towards the intruder. "I'll run away."

Dedda drank slowly. "Brave words, little one." He let Aunt Eliza take his empty glass. "What kind of future would you have with this youngster? There's no place without prejudice. Don't ruin your life, Leah, you'll end up all alone. We don't want to lose you, too." Dedda seemed to have expended all his remaining energy, closing his eyes and sighing deeply.

"Lia, no matter what he's saying, don't listen." Devraj implored. "Please, come with me, now."

No one acknowledged his words.

Through eyes, which prickled with tears, Lia glared at him. "I-I told you how important my studies are—"

"No more college." Dedda laid his head back against the armchair. His firm tone and stare gave her hope he was out of danger.

But the lethal words sank in and she felt faint. "But we agreed—"

"I'm sure Howard won't stand in your way. He's a good man." Dedda said, glancing at Devraj, his meaning clear; Howard was the right, Jewish man, while Devraj was forever an outsider.

"What's he saying, damn it?" Devraj demanded.

Lia watched her grandfather through tear-filled eyes until Devraj pulled her arm to face him. "You can't marry anyone else. How can you let anyone touch you the way I—"

Lia shoved his hand away and struck him hard across his face. The blow and her fury, almost throwing him off balance, seemed to stun everyone.

"You self-centred, arrogant bully. Not everything's about *you*." Her shrill words reverberated against the kitchen walls. "You've ruined my life."

How could three minutes destroy everything?

She'd lost her head for a moment, almost forgetting Devraj's father and his words, echoed by her grandparents right now.

Now Lia knew marrying Howard was her sole missile that would destroy Devraj's love for her forever. She'd have to sacrifice her future as she'd dreamed it, for Devraj's sake.

Dev's heart nearly shot out of his chest as Lia hung her head. He didn't need to understand the foreign language to know he'd never get through to these elders.

"Please, Lia, don't listen to their emotional blackmail." He was about to grasp her shoulders, but she evaded his touch.

"Don't you touch me." She said through gritted teeth as if she loathed looking at him. He knew she'd never forgive him now.

When she'd struck him, he felt her hot emotions running deeper than self-preservation. He wanted to hold her, to make it all better, but he couldn't take the old man over the edge. "I'm telling you again; I'll take care of you. Choose *us*, Lia. We'll manage. We don't need anyone else. I'll work—"

"You need money to survive, and you need family." Dedda said slowly, emphasising every word.

Devraj ignored him. "The most important thing is that we love each other."

"No, it's not." Lia pushed at him, anger and fear warring within her large eyes again.

"Are they going on about the security this guy offers?" he frowned. "What does Howard do?"

"It doesn't matter." Lia said through gritted teeth.

"He's a doctor." Lia's petite grandmother piped up.

"A doctor, no less. An established career, and looks much older than I." He stared at her grandparents, "You must be over the moon." Then back at Lia. "Heals people, has a great bedside manner. I can't compete with that."

Jealousy spurred him on, desperation of losing her escalated. He couldn't imagine living another day without her, while Lia couldn't bear to look at him.

He leaned closer. "You're a bloody coward," he accused, "selling yourself. Is he promising you can finish your degree and you'll travel together? Or will he want you barefoot and pregnant immediately?" The thought of her carrying another man's child almost blinded him.

Lia's suddenly ashen face stopped his next words. He'd been about to ask if this guy was expecting a fresh young virgin, but seeing Lia's earlier fury replaced with horror, he suddenly understood what he was up against.

Her imploring expression told him she was terrified to hurt, or even kill her grandparents, if not their remaining love for her.

"You really mean to go through with this madness?"

With desolate darkness within her eyes she said, "I'm going to marry Howard. Now get out of my life and stay away. I'll never forgive you." She averted her teary eyes, her every word like a fatal bullet to his heart, their finality killing any hope he'd harbored.

His chest hurt so deeply he couldn't breathe.

All energy drained from him.

Five impulsive minutes had lost Lia forever—and pushed her into another man's arms.

Shoulders slumped, he closed his eyes from the pain in hers. She was more afraid of losing her family than losing *him*. Yet he knew she loved him. Would she come to her senses before it was too late?

Slowly turning to leave, someone called his name. The silent woman, whom he guessed to be Lia's aunt, stood behind him. Her wise eyes were full of empathy.

He felt her firm grip on his shoulder as they left Lia and the grandparents behind. Turning his head back, he took one last look at his Lia in the tiny, stifling house. The growing lump in his throat almost strangled him. At least death would stop this agony.

"I'm so sorry for what you're going through," she said as they reached the front door. "But if you love Lia, and I believe you truly do, then let her go. She cannot do what you ask of her. It's not in her nature."

Tears blinded him. He turned away from the only person who genuinely seemed to comprehend his turmoil.

Without glancing back, he marched out of Lia's life. He had to trust in their destiny. It had to bring her back to him.

Epilogue

North London, June 1995

LEAVING THE TOMB-LIKE silence of the Rolls Royce, Lia gripped the heavy skirt of her imprisoning wedding dress, while accepting the stooping, old man's help to brave the summer downpour.

The big, bat-like umbrella over them absorbed the mini bullets of the rain, turning the pure white of her gown to gunmetal gray.

Was it sunrise or sunset? She couldn't remember. The universe had lost all color and warmth.

Her feet and heart refused to cooperate as the old man tightened his embrace around her and urged her toward the arched doors of the imposing granite-grey building ahead of them.

A familiar magnetic pull made her turn her head to look over her shoulder, across the road. Lips trembling under the stifling veil, she saw the soaking, unshaven, Devraj standing by his car.

She felt his agony, heard his thoughts, *How can you throw away your life, our destiny? Please come back to me!*

But the sleek, dark river of the London street may as well have been oceans separating them, like a chasm of culture neither could overcome.

Even if she was making the mistake of a lifetime, she needed him to see her enter the house of her God. Her first love was an illusion and a part of her past, now. He had to be.

Suddenly, thunder reverberated above them. She turned away from the love of her life. *Look forward, not back.*

"Love will come, you'll see. Howard will make you happy." Her grandmother's mantra over the past endless weeks had almost made Lia want to scream that it would only make her grandparents happy. But... here she was, still walking in the opposite direction from Devraj. For his own sake.

Whether or not he ever forgave her, one day she'd be proud of her strength and sacrifice.

Tears streaming down her face, she forced her legs up the stairs into the dimness. The cool, musty scent of the traditions ingrained into the spirit of the synagogue made her shiver.

Faces of curious strangers watched her advance towards the waiting bridegroom. The high jewel-tone stained-glass windows, to which generations of proud families had contributed, seemed about to shatter in on her. And, as every hesitant step led her closer to the man at the end of the aisle, his patent happiness made her steps falter, and she wanted to shout, *it's a lie, you know nothing about me!*

She almost stumbled, but Dedda supported her. The nightmare continued.

But *this* was her destiny, not the heart-broken, young man out in the rain.

Statue-still, she lowered her burning eyes behind the veil. If Devraj ran up that aisle, demanding he was her rightful soul mate, would she flee with him? No!

Sucking in a shaky breath, she prayed for strength from the same God who'd gifted—and then snatched away—an alternate, impossible future.

Anchoring her limbs, she swore to be the perfect wife to the smiling man beside her. She wasn't marrying him for her grandparents, but for a much bigger reason.

Or—she raised her head, heart pounding—she could grab the long train of her white dress as restrictive as armor, and escape into the arms of her one and only true love.

She took another fortifying breath. Her fingers unfurled from their fists like opening petals.

No. She couldn't go through with this.

If she married anyone, it would be Devraj.

As the cantor stopped singing his holy lyrics to the poignant music, and the Rabbi opened his mouth, Lia swiftly pulled away the veil and the crown off her head and threw it to the ground. Her heart thumping hard, she grabbed her skirt with both hands and turned away from the gaping Howard, and refused to look at her grandparents.

Whereas a few moments ago she was numb and unable to walk, she was now all motion and movement.

Among the gasps and shocked voices rumbling through the congregation, Lia bolted up the aisle so fast she prayed she wouldn't fall flat on her face.

Reaching the huge doors she pulled one cold handle towards herself and the slight screeching of the door made her take in another deep breath. Then she raced down the stairs and stopped on the dark wet asphalt. The icy rain dancing loudly off the ground instantly soaked her and her cumbersome dress.

Devraj's car suddenly shifted from its parked space and she choked out, "Oh, no..." She was too breathless to scream.

Breaking into a clumsy sprint, with the freezing silk swooshing around and between her legs she forced herself to run on to the thankfully quiet street. But Devraj's car roared away from her with every second.

She shrieked his name out and it reverberated around her with the booming thunder and the clattering rain.

Uncaring about being soaked through, all she could do was pray that Devraj heard her or saw her in his rear view mirror. The screeching sounds of his breaks made her release a long held breath and as his car came to a halt, she escaped towards her destiny.

She shot towards him, blinking away her tears and the rain, then the laughing, running Devraj was holding out his arms ready to catch her and hold her forever.

What's Coming Up Next?

A Happily-ever-after! Lia and Devraj deserve it.

But, wait, what if this story *doesn't* end here? What if Devraj and Lia cannot fulfill their destiny and their happy-ever-after is stolen from them?

Well, then you may enjoy reading their continuing and final story in SECOND DESTINY, when they reunite nineteen years later, and their sizzling attraction for each other and their reignited passion overtakes *everything*.

About the Author

Ever since she was little, Gloria Silk knew that creating and sharing her romantic stories with others, was her passion. She always loved reading contemporary and historical novels that grasped her imagination. After many years of running art and design related businesses and being a published non-fiction author under a different name, Gloria now writes intense, sensuous love stories full-time.

Her special interests are in intercultural romances and family bonds. What can be more important in life than love and family?

Born in Russia, Gloria Silk has visited and lived in amazing, exotic places, including some in Europe and the Mediterranean. Her favorite in the world, by far is Hawaii.

Being a writer gives her the privilege to explore, travel, and meet wonderful, new and exciting—and sometimes eccentric—people. Her background in English literature, writing, and psychology helps her create unique characters for her stories. Especially the charismatic heroes and feisty heroines who find themselves in sticky situations with each other, their families, and their cultures. There is nothing more satisfying than knowing readers love her warm heroines and the gorgeous enigmatic heroes, like *she* falls in love with them.

When she is not painting in various media or watching romantic movies, or cooking up a storm for her family and friends, she hangs out with her writing friends and other creatives.

Although she was brought up in England, she now lives—and writes—in the Toronto suburbs in Ontario, Canada, with her husband and teenage daughter.

If you enjoyed this book please consider reviewing it and telling your friends about it. Gloria Silk would also love to hear from you. Contact her through her website, www.GloriaSilk.com and she will notify you about her next book releases. Partial proceeds of all Gloria Silk's book sales go to Canadian Cancer Society.

* 9 7 8 0 9 9 3 6 9 5 2 3 0 *